Charles Cte de Montalembert

Memoir of the Abbé Lacordaire

Charles Cte de Montalembert

Memoir of the Abbé Lacordaire

ISBN/EAN: 9783337094164

Printed in Europe, USA, Canada, Australia, Japan

Cover: Foto ©Andreas Hilbeck / pixelio.de

More available books at **www.hansebooks.com**

MEMOIR

OF THE

ABBÉ LACORDAIRE

BY

THE COUNT DE MONTALEMBERT,

ONE OF THE FORTY OF THE FRENCH ACADEMY.

AUTHORIZED TRANSLATION.

RICHARD BENTLEY,

PUBLISHER IN ORDINARY TO HER MAJESTY.

1863.

LONDON:

PRINTED BY GEORGE PHIPPS, 13 & 14, TOTHILL STREET,
WESTMINSTER.

TRANSLATOR'S PREFACE.

WE live in an age not indifferent to, although not prolific in, individual greatness. The race of those giants of olden times, whose stately forms stand out upon the dim horizon of history and awe us, seems to have died out.

To account for this would involve a difficult but interesting study. The most we can do is to endeavour to perpetuate the memory of those among us who come nearest to this ideal. The subject of this Memoir seems to have been of this cast. England has her likes and her dislikes, her shortcomings and her prejudices; but, of all the nations of the earth she is, perhaps, the one which, in a sound, common-sense kind of way, without any feverish enthusiasm, knows how to appreciate and honor manly virtue. She has fought her way slowly up to the liberty which is to-day her glory and her pride. She reveres and loves the men who, from generation to generation, have handed down to her the accumulated fruit of toil and trial, of sacrifice and strife. She is, consequently, not indifferent to the struggles of those who in every country have trodden, or are still treading, the same thorny path.

It is for this reason that we think the present work will interest the English public.

That LACORDAIRE was one of these men is beyond a doubt. He lived at a time when the clergy were looked down upon in France. He left the bar where a brilliant future awaited him, and became a priest. He fought for liberty; he was for twenty years the idol of the French youth. He was one of the greatest of modern orators. He was sent to represent France in

the National Assembly at a time when the frock
of the monk was looked upon with anything but
favor.

Finally, the French Academy opened its ranks
to him. All this is more than sufficient to prove
that he was no ordinary man.

A life of Lacordaire written especially for the
English public would have been a very desirable
work. It would have offered a very good picture
of France during the last thirty years.* Count
de Montalembert has written for his countrymen
the book which we submit to the English public.
It would undoubtedly have rendered the task of
any one attempting a life of Lacordaire a difficult
one. The concentrated power, the eloquence, the
high-minded frankness displayed in this book,

---

* A volume of the Letters of Lacordaire has recently
been published in Paris, where they have been received
with enthusiasm. Should the present Work be found accept-
able to English readers, these Letters will follow the present
publication.

have rendered it deservedly popular in France. It is like one of those rapid sketches by the old masters, in which a few powerful strokes of the pencil present to the looker-on the living, breathing individual. We offer it to the English public fearful, as translators must generally be, lest the original may have somewhat suffered in the transfer ; but conscious, at the same time, that we have endeavoured to render faithfully a very beautiful sketch.

There is an allusion in the book which to contemporaries of the time spoken of by the Count de Montalembert will present no difficulty, but which younger readers would not understand without a few preliminary remarks. We shall give them as concisely as possible. The allusion is that made to M. de la Mennais. The Count supposes his history to be familiar to the reader.

Félicité de la Mennais was born at St. Malo in 1780. Whilst still young he had made a name as a writer. In 1817, he published the first

volume of his *Essay upon Indifference* in matters of religion. It immediately placed him in
the first rank of European thinkers and writers.
Three years later he published the second volume,
in which he propounded and defended an entirely
novel theory upon *certitude*. This volume was
followed by a *Defence* of the Essay, and then
by the third and fourth volumes. The clergy of
France were greatly divided upon the views taken
in this work. The consequences deduced from
the system of de la Mennais were condemned,
first by the majority of the French bishops, and
secondly by the Encyclical letter of Gregory
XVI. of August 15th, 1832. This is the great
man whose story is so graphically told by the
Count de Montalembert in this book. He died
in Paris a few years ago.

The author of this Work requires no intro-
duction to the English public, or indeed to the
public of any quarter of the civilized world.
The name of the Count de Montalembert has

for the last twenty years been as familiar to us as that of any of our own statesmen or writers. Birth, talent, eloquence, courage, and purpose, were entrusted to him for the furthering of the great cause of liberty, religious and civil. He has turned them to noble account. He is one of the few who are stronger than defeat. His voice has not been heard in the French House for several years. France has sustained this loss because of his magnanimous opposition to a school of politicians who were in high favor with a large section of the French clergy, and who are well described in the latter portion of this book. We may hope that the coming elections will put France and Europe once more in possession of a voice which has ever been the organ of all that is generous, pure, noble, and great.

May 16, 1868.

CONTENTS.

————◆————

PAGE

CHAPTER I. 1

What he was, and what we have lost.—The Albigensian
woman's opinion of Lacordaire.—Confers honor on
France.—Born a democrat.—Opinion of rationalism.
—Sympathy.

CHAPTER II. 12

Publication of *L'Avenir.*—Daniel O'Connell.—Abbé de la
Mennais.—The appearance of Lacordaire.—The Con-
vent of Visitandines.—Parentage.—Opinions.—The
Priest of Aubusson refuses burial to a certain person.
—Lacordaire's opinion of the priest.—Church and
State.—Brought before the Correctional Police.—Is
indicted by Louis Philippe's Government.—His de-

fence.—The French Charta.—Charges the Government.—His acquittal.—The Trial of the Free School.
—Conflict with Government.—Summoned before the
House of Peers.—Defends himself.—Impression made
upon the Peers.—M. de Laprade.—Journey to Rome.
—Pope Gregory XVI.—Divergence of opinion between De la Mennais and Lacordaire.—Lacordaire
leaves Rome for France.—Goes to Germany.—Publication of Pope Gregory's Encyclical Letter.

CHAPTER III.   65

Retires into Brittany.—Rupture with M. de la Mennais.—
M. de la Mennais' disappointment.—Publication of
Affaires de Rome.—Lacordaire's criticism on it.—
Explanation of his conduct in separating from M. de
la Mennais.—De la Mennais isolated.—His opinions.
—Lacordaire seeks Count Montalembert, and com-
bats the opinions of De la Mennais.

CHAPTER IV.   89

Solitary life of Lacordaire.—Outbreak of the cholera.—
Desire for a good and obscure life.—Madame Swet-
chine.—Her influence upon Lacordaire.—His life in
Paris.—Fails in his early efforts as a preacher.—

PAGE

Assists at the Collège Stanislas.—Preaches at Notre-
Dame.—Archbishop Quelen.

CHAPTER V. 109

Retirement of Lacordaire.—Second visit to Rome.—
Contemplates entering the Dominican Order.—
Preaches on the Vocation of the French Nation.—
Resides at Bosco in Piedmont.—Liberty of Educa-
tion.—The University Party.—Archbishop Affre.—
Liberty of Association.—Dupanloup, Bishop of Or-
leans, on the spirit of the French Revolution.—
Popularity of Lacordaire.

CHAPTER VI. 141

Self-denial of Lacordaire.—Excessive rigours of his
penance.—His eloquence.—Sermons on Our Saviour.
—Description of Lacordaire.—His power as an extempore preacher.—Comparison with Bossuet.—
Nature of his acquirements.—His taste.—Pretended
conversion of Napoleon at St. Helena.—Specimens
of Lacordaire's eloquence.—His comprehension of
love.—The love of the husband.—The love of the
father.—M. Scherer's criticism rebuked.

PAGE

CHAPTER VII.   178

Character of Lacordaire. —Erroneous judgments respect-
ing him.—Lacordaire's mode of meeting them.—
Accused of violence and passion.—Montalembert's
defence.—Lacordaire's character and qualities.—His
hopefulness.—His trust.—Judgment and prudence.
—His moderation.—Funeral oration by Cardinal
Donnet.—His power of conciliating modern ideas
with old truths.—Combats Papal Omnipotence.—
Charity of Lacordaire.

CHAPTER VIII.   207

Lacordaire's political life.—Not fond of politics.—His
political attitude.—The new society.—Conduct of
Lacordaire in the face of the Revolution of 1848.—
The Italian War.—Becomes a member of the Constituent Assembly, but retires in ten days.—Retires
from the Editorship of the *Ere Nouvelle.*—Address
at Notre-Dame to the Archbishop of Paris.—Nobleness of Lacordaire's character.—The Italian War
of 1859.—Lacordaire's altered views.—The Roman
Question.—The Liberty of the Italian Church.—
Lacordaire's letter to Guizot on the publication of
Guizot's *Church and Christian Society* in 1861.

PAGE

CHAPTER IX. 247

Lacordaire's last conferences at Notre-Dame.—Farewell address.—Apostrophe to Notre-Dame.—Sermon in favor of the Ecoles Chrétiennes.—The First Napoleon and Pope Pius VII.—The Spanish War.—Goes to Toulouse.—His conferences there.—Has finally to give up preaching in public.—Becomes Director of the School of Sorèze.—France of to-day.—Severe judgment upon European statesmanship.—The Ultramontane School.—Its conduct under the second empire.—Attitude of the French Clergy.—Lacordaire desires the hatred of the Ultramontanists.—Life at Sorèze.—Elected to the French Academy.—Love of children.—His last Lent.—His devotion to his duties. —The aim of life.—Desires to publish a body of apologetic and moral theology.—Adopts one of his pupils at Sorèze.—Chateaubriand at Venice.—Contentedness of Lacordaire.—His last hours.—His future fame.

LACORDAIRE.

CHAPTER I.

"*Abion un rey, l'aben perdut :*" "We had a king, "and we have lost him," exclaimed, in her Albigensian dialect, a good woman from among the twenty thousand Christians assembled at Sorèze to pay magnificent and popular homage to the remains of Lacordaire. This cry of artless admiration, mingled with grief, faithfully depicts the emotion now uppermost in every heart which has either directly or indirectly undergone the influence of Lacordaire.

B

But how shall we express what those must feel
who have lived of his life, who have followed this
star from the first dawn of its brightness to its
splendid decline?

In endeavouring to speak of him I experience
still more embarrassment than sorrow. Silence
alone would seem to become a great grief, especially when mingled with great respect. He it is,
I think, who one day said to me, "How powerless
"is man for his fellow man! Of all his miseries
"this is the deepest." Never did I more keenly
feel the truth of this remark than in presence of
the task imposed upon me of rendering a super-
fluous homage to him whom so many men have
loved, whom I too loved so strongly, and who
so devotedly loved my soul.

I am but too certain beforehand not to do justice to this great, pure, and well-employed life.
It has then drawn to a close,—that life which
seemed to us the most precious, the most necessary of all! He is dead, but we are all stricken:
"His death dwarfs us all," said Arago at the
grave of Cuvier. Of the old friends and young
disciples of Lacordaire we may say more: we lie

about this prostrate oak, some crushed, others
uprooted, all stunned by its fall.

Alas ! we have lost far more than a king.
The Gospel says, that the mother who has brought
forth thinks no more of her anguish, because
a man is born into the world, " *Quia natus*
" *est homo in mundum.*" And we are deso-
late because a man is lost to the world ; yes,
above all, a real man ! and what a man ! Is it
too much to say that he was one of the greatest
orators, one of the greatest religious, one of
the greatest servants of God who have appeared
during this century ? Surely not ; and I may
add, without fear of hurting his most illustrious
rivals, that neither among the dead nor the
living of our time will history discover a more
singular and more attractive personage. This
orator, this religious, this liberal who has been
among us the descendant and the worthy repre-
sentative of St. Dominic, Bossuet, and O'Connell, belongs to all the great families of human
thought. He belongs, above all, to that race of
rare and strong-minded men, who, born on the
confines of two centuries, have, despite faults and

weaknesses, redeemed France from her crimes, and raised her from the dust: who have honoured, served, and elevated the French mind, who have inaugurated, instead of the triumphs of the spirit of usurpation and conquest, a period of enlightenment, of liberty, of public and intellectual life, of Catholic regeneration.

The name of Lacordaire will pale before none of the great names which have presided at this great political and religious resurrection.

Born at the beginning of this century, he knew all its trials and all its greatness. Born a democrat, and nursed in republican ideas, he early circumscribed, without ever extinguishing it, that revolutionary lava which from time to time burst forth in his discourses, no longer to spread ruin and dismay, but to serve as a beacon in the surrounding night.

When he became a believer, a Catholic, a priest, and a monk, he betrayed no single one of the rightful instincts and generous convictions of his youth.

He reminds us of one of those barbarians whom the maternal hand of the Church used to

seek out from amidst those hostile and victorious
hordes, the terror of her children, to make them
apostles. Once baptized, anointed, and consecrated by her, without ever laying aside anything
of their native energy, they became, like St.
Martin, St. Boniface, or St. Columbanus, all powerful mediators between her and a new world, and
brought over to her crowds of faithful born
out of her bosom, born to fight against her,
but suddenly changed into docile champions of
the truth : "*Miraturque novas frondes, et non
sua poma.*"

This Christian Achilles, imbued from his cradle with, and given heart and soul to, modern
ideas, thus steeled against the regrets and ties
of the past, emerged from this Stygian lake to
be enamoured of the soul alone, to fix his gaze
during forty years upon heaven, and to show its
road to generations gone astray.

He was undoubtedly the most striking per-
sonification in the Church of this new spirit, which
Christians are inexorably condemned to adopt and
to employ, under penalty of leaving truth de-
fenceless and fettered upon unknown shores.

And yet, sad and strange to say, he, the greatest of priests, and the purest of democrats, was never adopted by democracy,* nor ever thoroughly understood and appreciated by the clergy.

" Speak out then, you who have been the wit-
" ness of his life;" are the words that meet my

---

* To show the account to which publicity is turned amongst us, be it said that a French paper (*Le Temps* of Nov. 24, 1861) has been found to accuse Lacordaire, (and this paper goes to the trouble of putting its assertion between inverted commas, and quoting the date,) of having in 1838 called human reason the "daughter of nothing," " a power which, originating in the " demon, is incompatible with faith, which is of God." The expressions quoted, and distorted in the quotation, were ap- plied by Lacordaire to *rationalism*, and not to reason. Indeed, in the only publication of his, which appeared in 1838, he says that all rationalists are not of the same sort. Lacordaire, who said that reason was the *sister* of faith, is decidedly of all Christian orators the one who has most extolled and patronized human reason.

This ridiculous calumny immediately found a thousand echoes, especially in England, by means of a widely circulated periodical (*Saturday Review*, Nov. 30, 1861). This publi- cation adds, on its own account, that Lacordaire is the type of a species which is "only not monstrous because so very ludicrous."

ear. "As far as he is concerned posterity already "exists : tell us what you know of him."

Yes, I acknowledge it; I can be this witness ; and satisfied as I am that he will attain the summit of his renown only in a century hence, I cannot refuse my evidence. Before leaving in our turn this earth where it is so painful to outlive our friends, it is but right to do what in us lies to help history in the formation of that verdict, which we must both expect and dread, although it is neither universal nor infallible.

I shall then contribute what I believe to be independent and unbiassed evidence. It is true that if not my master, he was my friend ; but thirty years are more than sufficient to dispel every illusion, to shake off the dreams of imagination, and purify the fire of enthusiasm.

Moreover, we have not always agreed. Ever one at heart, we differed in mind ; ever unanimous upon the object to be attained, we frequently differed upon the course to be adopted.

These very divergencies leave me free to contemplate him without being dazzled, and to praise without flattering him.

Of all the great points which his life offers,
I am chiefly desirous of showing what was his
character, what the quality of his soul. In the
first place I will praise him for having remained
true to himself, without a moment's wavering,
throughout the whole of his career ; for having,
under so many different governments, and in the
midst of universal defection "been always equally
" mindful of his soul and his honour," and for
having given an immortal example of unwavering
steadfastness. Without ever striking his colours,
he was able to hold out his hand to all honest men
who were not his brethren in the faith, because
he remained himself, above all, an honest man ;
that is, a man accessible to all, respected by all,
and such as he himself so well defined him in one
of the last outbursts of his victorious eloquence.

"I am," he exclaimed, " a Christian, and that
" is the reason why I am moved at the idea of
" an honest man. I picture to myself the vene-
" rable type of a man whose heart has never con-
" ceived, and whose hand has never perpetrated
" injustice. . . . . A man of his word, faithful in
" friendship ; sincere and firm in his conviction ;

"above the influence of time, which changes
"everything, and bears away everything with its
"changes; a man alike removed from obstinacy
"in error, and from that insolence peculiar to
"apostacy, which bespeaks either the meanness
"of treason, or the shameful fickleness of incon-
"stancy. . . . . . . This is not exactly the type
"of the hero, but it is something noble, and per-
"haps, alas! something but too rarely found
"in its perfection. Whatever and whoever you
"may be, a good Christian, yea! even a saint,
"reverence and love the voice which whispers
"to you in the depths of your conscience, you
"are an honest man!"

I shall endeavour to lay open in its true light,
even more so than his character, that soul which,
like Almighty God, did love our souls above all
things: "*Domine qui amas animas;*"* that soul
in which austerity and firmness were blended with
such a wonderful sweetness, in which tenderness

---

* Sap. xi. 27.

and loftiness went hand in hand, in which the
candour of the child was allied to such intense
manliness. He was one of those to whom, as
Bossuet says, "The light of reason and the
" honour of liberty are no burthen."*

But he was also one of those who naturally
lean upon the heart of another; who have that
boundless sympathy for others' weaknesses, which
he himself used to call "kindheartedness," and
which he preferred to everything else. The remembrance of that disposition in him encourages
me to sketch a narrative which will scarcely be
more than the tear of a Friend. Let others
pay tribute to his genius, his holiness, his brilliant oratory, his great works; beneath the powerful writer, the incomparable orator, the austere
religious, my weakness will seek out the man,
and in the man, that pure and generous, that
tender and intrepid heart, which for thirty years,
I have felt beating like my own.

And for this purpose it shall be less I than he

---

* Sermon on the grounds of Divine Vengeance.

himself who will speak. He shall himself show us how in kindliness there is, "besides the gra-
" tuitous gift of oneself, a certain way of giving
" oneself, a charm which conceals the gift, a
" transparency which discloses the heart and
" makes us love it, a peculiar simplicity, sweet-
" ness, and delicate attentiveness which attracts
" the whole man, and makes him prefer a kind
" and loving soul even to genius itself."*

---

* Panegyric of the B. P. Fourier.

CHAPTER II.

THE JOURNAL "L'AVENIR."—THE TRIAL OF THE
FREE-SCHOOL.—JOURNEY TO ROME.

I saw him for the first time in the closet of
the Abbé de la Mennais, in November 1830, four
months after a revolution, beneath whose ruins the
throne and the altar seemed for a moment to be
buried,* and one month after the first appearance

---

* On the 25th of July, 1830, King Charles X. published
the *Ordonnances*, by which he introduced, without the consent
of the two Chambers of Parliament, several important alterations in the laws relating to elections, and to the freedom of
the press. Although these alterations left France in possession
of an infinitely greater amount of political freedom than her

of the paper *L'Avenir*. The motto of this paper was "*God and Liberty.*" It was meant, according to the views of its founders, to regenerate Catholic opinion in France, and to cement the union between it and liberal progress. I hastened to share in this work with the ardour of my twenty years, from the west of Ireland, where I had just seen O'Connell at the head of a people whose invincible attachment to the Catholic faith had weathered three centuries of persecution, and whose religious emancipation had just been achieved by freedom of the press and of speech. A small number of laymen and a still smaller number of priests had taken up M. de la Mennais' idea. Among the latter the Abbé Lacordaire, as yet unknown, was mentioned to me. Not only was he not one of those who had made a name by retailing the doctrines of the

---

present condition admits of, the people of Paris rose in insurrection, and after three days' fighting, a revolution took place, which ended in the accession to the throne of the Duke d'Orléans, under the name of King Louis Philippe.—[*Translator's Note.*]

celebrated author of the *Essay upon Indifference,* but he was in no sense his pupil. He
wrote on the 7th of June, 1825, "I like neither
"the system of M. de la Mennais, which I
"believe to be unsound, nor his political opinions,
"which seem to me exaggerated." Subsequently
a few days passed at La Chesnaie brought him
into closer connexion with the great polemist,
who had become as revolutionary as he had been
monarchical, and who remained as extravagant
and unyielding in his republicanism as he had
been in his royalism. But nothing less than the
revolution of July and the *Avenir* could have
coupled in one common work these two widely
dissimilar natures.

I saw them both together for the first time;
dazzled and mastered by the one, I felt myself
more gently and naturally drawn towards the
other. Who will give me to portray him as he
then appeared to me in all the strength and
bloom of youth! He was twenty-eight years of
age; dressed as a layman, (the state of Paris
rendering the wearing of the ecclesiastical cos-
tume impossible,) his tall, slight frame, his fine

regular features, his beautifully chiselled forehead, the already royal sit of his head, his dark flashing eye, a certain lofty elegance subdued by a modesty noticeable in his whole person ; all this was but the outer garment of a soul which seemed ready to overflow, not only in the tourneys of public speech, but in the confidential out-pourings of intimacy. His brilliant eye bespoke at the same time treasures of anger and tenderness : it seemed to be on the look-out not only for enemies to combat and overthrow, but for hearts to conquer and win. His voice, already so firm and vibrating, assumed at times a tone of infinite sweetness. Born for strife and for love, his whole being already bespoke the two-fold empire of soul and talent. He appeared to me bewitching and terrible, the type of enthusiasm in the cause of good, of virtue armed for truth. I saw in him a chosen one, predestined to all that youth most adores and covets—genius and glory. But he, more charmed by the sweet joys of Christian friendship than by the distant echoes of renown, showed me that the greatest struggles but half move us ; that they leave us strength enough to live above all the life of the heart; that days begin and end according as a cherished memory awakes or subsides in the soul. It was he who thus spoke to me; adding immediately, " Alas! we ought to " love the infinite alone, and that is why when " we do love, that which we love is so infinitely " accomplished in our soul."

On the morrow after our first meeting, he took me to hear his mass, which he said in the chapel of a little convent of Visitandines, in the *Quartier Latin;* * and we already loved each other, as people are wont to love in the pure and generous outpourings of youth, and under the fire of the enemy.

He condescended to enjoy this connection which he had wished for, and on which he congratulated himself in terms akin to his classical and democratic ideas. Shortly before he wrote,

---

* So called because the schools of law, medicine, the Sorbonne, &c. &c., are here.

"My soul, like Iphigenia, awaits my brother at the foot of the altar." Then talking of his newly made friend to an older one he said : "I love him "as if he were a Plebeian."*

Nothing can be conceived more simple and commonplace than the early life of this young priest. Those who, in the lives of historical personages, or at least in the accounts of their youth, look for romance and storms, must betake themselves elsewhere.† No adventures, no stroke of chance, or outburst of passion disturbed the course of his youth.

The son of a village doctor, brought up by a pious mother, he had, like nearly all the young men of that day, lost his faith at college, and recovered it neither in the law schools, nor at the

---

* Lorain, *Biographie du Père Lacordaire, Correspondant,* vol. xviii., p. 19.

† For everything relative to the youth of Lacordaire, see the excellent and interesting notice published in the *Correspondant,* in 1847, (vols. xvii. and xviii.,) by M. Lorain, one of his old friends and schoolfellows. It contains many of his letters.

C

bar, where he remained two years among the Sta-
giarian* barristers.

Nothing, apparently, marked him out from
among his fellows; he was a deist like all the
youth of his day, he was a liberal like almost
every Frenchman of that time, but without any
extreme views.

He shared in the convictions and the generous
illusions which we all breathed in the air cleared
by the downfall of imperial despotism. He ad-
vocated, however, nothing but a strong and
lawful liberty, and although devoid, as yet, of the
light of faith, he already perceived the greatest
danger threatening modern society, for at twenty
years of age he wrote, " Impiety begets depravity.
" Corrupt morals beget corrupt laws, and licence
" forges the fetters of nations." He himself was
always pure and regular in his morals : his only

------

* A term used to designate young barristers, who in France
are expected, during the three years following their call to the
bar, to assist at the cases tried in court, to meet at certain
times for conferences, at which the avocat bâtonnier (senior
barrister) presides, and accept such briefs as may be assigned
to them by the president of the court.

passion was that of glory. Even before becoming a believer, he respected himself. He needed not to leave the path of disorder, for he never knew it. Even then he said, " I am sated, without " having bought satiety by experience." He frequently repeated that neither man nor book was the instrument of his conversion. A sudden and secret stroke of grace opened his eyes to the nothingness of irreligion. In a single day he became a believer, and once a believer he wished to become a priest. A seminarist at S. Sulpice* in 1824, ordained priest in 1827, a convent chaplain in 1828, and a college chaplain in 1829, nothing seemed to mark him out from the ordinary run of men.

The only singularity about him was his liberalism. By a phenomenon, at that time unheard of, this convert, this seminarist, this confessor of nuns, was just as stubborn a liberal as in the days when he was but a student and barrister.

----

* The chief Ecclesiastical Seminary of the diocese of Paris and of all France.

" I am unwilling," he said, " to forego, as a
" believer, those ideas of order, justice, strong
" and lawful liberty, which were my first con-
" quests. Christianity is not a law of bondage.
" . . . . . . It has not forgotten that its children
" were free at a time when the world was groaning
" in fetters under a series of brutal emperors, and
" that they had formed beneath the earth a society
" which spoke of humanity under the palace of
" Nero. . . . . The Church had the words
" reason and liberty on her lips, when the im-
" prescriptible rights of the human race were
" threatened with shipwreck. . . . ."*

He consequently understood in his youth, and
in solitude, that of which those around him did
not appear to have a glimpse : first of all, that
the Church, after having given liberty to the
modern world, was, in her turn, right as well as
bound to claim that liberty ; and secondly, that
she could no longer ask for it as a privilege, but

---

* Letter to M. Lorain, p. 833.

simply as her share in the common patrimony of modern society.

M. de la Mennais, at that time the most celebrated as well as the most venerated of the French clergy, starting from the opposite extreme, had worked his way to the same conclusion. This was the reason of his connexion with the obscure chaplain of the College Henri IV.* Such was the ground upon which both planted the banner of the *Avenir.* Neither the old clergy nor the new government were inclined to relish this new doctrine; but the awkwardness and violence of the latter might be relied upon in order to enlighten and bring round the former.

Then came the double duty of showing up the arbitrary acts of certain functionaries against religion, and of teaching Catholics to look to liberal institutions and ideas for weapons which the fall of a dynasty should no longer be able to snap asunder in their hands.

---

* Now styled *Lycée Napoléon.*

It was to this double task that the young Henry Lacordaire devoted his yet unripe and hitherto completely unknown talents. At the very outset he equalled, and, in fact, eclipsed the fiery eloquence of the great writer whose disciple he wrongly believed himself to be.

A few days after our first meeting, I read in the *Avenir* an article bearing the initials of that name now destined to publicity. The point in question was the refusal to bury a certain person by the parish priest of Aubusson ; after which, the sub-prefect of that place had introduced into the church, by armed force, the remains of a man who had died without asking for the sacraments. The priest Lacordaire mentioned it, and spoke of it to the other priests of France in the following terms :—

" One of your brothers has refused to a man " deceased, without your communion, the words " and prayers of Christian farewell. . . . . " Your brother has done well. He has behaved " like a free man, like a priest of God, resolved " to keep his lips from servile blessings. Woe " to him who blesses against the voice of his

" conscience, who speaks of God with a venal
" heart. Woe to the priest who mutters lies over
" a coffin ! who ushers in souls to the judgment
" of God for fear of the living, and for a vile
" coin !

" Your brother has done well. Are we the
" grave-diggers of the human race ? have we en-
" tered into a compact with it to flatter its remains ?
" more unfortunate than courtiers, who at the death
" of a prince are free to treat him as his life de-
" served. Your brother has done well ; but a dwarf
" of a pro-consul was of opinion that such an
" amount of independence did not become so hum-
" ble a citizen as a Catholic priest. He ordered
" the body to be laid before the altar, even if
" violence should be needed to effect this purpose,
" —even should it be necessary to force the doors
" of the temple, where, under the shield of laws of
" our country, and of liberty, rests the God of all
" men, and of the majority of the French nation.

" He has had his way ; a file of the National
" Guard carried the body into the Church ; brute
" force and death have violated the house of
" God, in time of peace, without even the excuse

" of a riot, by the orders of the administration.
" The house of a private citizen cannot be vio-
" lated without the intervention of law : and, in
" the present case, law was not even asked to
" say to religion, ' Veil thy face for a moment
" ' before my sword.'

  "A simple sub-prefect, a stipendiary remove-
" able at will, has, from his house where he sits,
" guarded against tyranny by thirty millions of
" men, sent a corpse into the temple of God.
" He has done this, whilst you were sleeping in
" peace upon the sworn faith of the Charter of
" the 7th of August,—whilst you were told to
" bless, in the person of the king, the key-
" stone of a great nation's liberties. He has
" done it in presence of a law which declares
" all religions to be free ;* and I ask what is
" the meaning of a free religion, if its temple,
" its altar, be not inviolable, if a corpse can

---

* Article 5th of the Charta, granted on June 9th, 1814, by
Louis XVIII., and amended on August 17th, 1830, by the
Parliament which proclaimed Louis Philippe.

" be ushered into it by armed violence ? He has
" done this wrong to the half of the French
" nation, he, that sub-prefect !

" Now the man who has bearded in their re-
" ligion so many Frenchmen, who has treated a
" place in which men bend their knee more irre-
" verently than he would have done had it been
" a stable,—this man is sitting by his fire-side,
" quiet, and satisfied with himself. His cheek
" would have blanched, if, staff in hand, you had
" carried your outraged God into some humble
" hut, vowing not to expose him a second time
" to the insults of state-temples."*

These last words foreshadowed the extreme,
unjust, and dangerous conclusion from which the
Avenir did not recoil. It flatly told the French
clergy that they must be prepared to give up
the State-grant, the only remnant of their ancient
and lawful patrimony, the only guarantee of their
material existence ; to give up even the churches,

---

* *Avenir*, Nov. 29th, 1830.

the ownership of which was claimed by the State, in order to enter upon the enjoyment of the invincible strength and inexhaustible resources of modern liberty. As for this liberty, he thus depicted its gorgeous charms to his astonished co-religionists :

" Can civil *censure* be to-day wielded by the " Church ?   No !   Can and will the State entrust " civil censure to the Church ?   No.   Liberty " then remains, and thank God for it.   God be " praised for having created man so noble a " creature that force in vain plots against his " mind, and that here below the only judge of " thought is thought !   Order, far from being " destroyed by free combat between error and " truth, finds, in this very· combat, its original " and universal condition.

" It might be urged against the Sovereign " Creator, that evil would be mightier than good " in the freedom which He chose to grant us. " He did, nevertheless, choose it, knowing that " free-will is the chief good, against which crime " cannot prevail, since crime is but a proof of " free-will.

" Besides, in no sense is it true that evil is
" stronger than good, and that truth is struggling
" upon the earth with arms whose weakness must
" be made up for by the aid of some absolute
" power. Were this the case, truth would be in
" a sorry plight ; for absolute power has never
" worked for any but its own ends. Was Chris-
" tianity founded by the help of absolute power ?
" Were the heresies of the Eastern empire over-
" thrown by the aid of absolute power ? Was it
" that power which converted the Arian peoples
" of the West ? Is it by the help of that power
" that the philosophy of the eighteenth century
" is now crumbling into dust ? Persecuted truth
" has always and everywhere triumphed over
" protected and powerful error. Such is the
" lesson of history. And to-day we are told
" that if truth is reduced to the necessity of
" fighting out its own cause, with its own arms,
" all is lost. What madness ! There is but one
" proof that everything here below is not a lie,
" and the play of the imagination, and that proof
" is that a thing hated from the beginning, wounded
" and bleeding from the beginning, has, never-

"theless, surmounted all human obstacles; and
" you imagine that this thing, for ever buffeted
" by the waves, will perish by liberty !

" Many are the men who have shaken their
" heads in passing before Christ, but, I tell you,
" I have met none in history whose blasphemy
" equals yours.   You do not know the Galileean.

" Catholics, believe me, let us leave to those,
" whose sole trust is in the princes of the earth,
" the hopes of serfdom.   Let us allow them to
" say that all is lost if the press be allowed full
" liberty, let them plunge into those lamentable
" conclusions where they will have to choose
" between the destruction of order and that of
" reason.   As for us, enlightened by the lengthy
" pilgrimage of our Church upon this earth, do
" not let us be so easily disconcerted; with our
" crucifix upon our breast, let us pray and
" struggle : days cannot undo ages, freedom will
" never kill God." *

* _Avenir_, June 12, 1831.

Thus wrote, with a singular mixture of youthful effervescence and powerful originality, this priest, this unknown youth of twenty-eight years! He did not stop here. He spoke as he wrote. He understood that in countries which have already won, or are still striving for freedom, great questions are always mooted, as at Rome and in England, in the noonday of judicial publicity. A series of contests, too long to be related here, which, however, all had in view the emancipation of the Catholic priest and citizen, brought him more than once before the Court of Correctional Police, either as defendant, in quality of civilian, or as counsel; for until he was prevented by the Council of Discipline, he pleaded in his capacity of barrister; and I remember the surprise of the president of the court upon finding one day at the bar, dressed in his barrister's gown, this priest, whose name was already beginning to attract notice.

The papers of that time would give us some fragments of his already manly eloquence, which bothered counsel and electrified the audience.

One day, when answering a certain crown-lawyer, who had ventured to say that Roman Catholic priests were the ministers of a foreign power, Lacordaire exclaimed, "We are the min- "isters of one who is a foreigner nowhere—of " God." Upon this the audience, mostly made " up of that people of Paris, so hostile to the clergy, began to cheer, and cried out to him, " Your name, young priest, your name, you are a " fine fellow!" He always had a certain hanker- ing after these conflicts : one would have said that he was trying the temper of his blade, as well as the sureness of his aim.

" I am convinced," he wrote, after one of these skirmishes, " that the Roman senate would not " unnerve me." And, in fact, no man ever seemed to suffer less from what he himself termed " the "agonies of public speaking."*

Government soon did him the service to open to him an arena worthier of his powers. The king, Louis Philippe, using for the first time a

---

* Notice upon Ozanam.

prerogative allowed by the Concordat, had just appointed three new bishops. Irritated, and not without reason, by two articles which imputed to it malevolent intentions, with an intemperance of language which, later on, Lacordaire acknowledged and regretted, Government indicted him, as well as M. de la Mennais, for incitement to contempt of Government, and disobedience to the laws. They appeared before the Court of Assize on 31st of January, 1831. M. de la Mennais was ably defended by M. Janvier. The Abbé Lacordaire acted as his own counsel; he moved even his judges, by engrafting on his bold doctrines a touching and modest allusion to himself. Our readers will be glad to have a few fragments of this speech, which has never been republished since 1831.

At the outset of his speech, he said : " I rise " with a thought which will never leave me. For- " merly, when the priest rose in the midst of the " people, a something which excited deep affec- " tion rose with his person. To-day, defendant " though I be, I know that my title as a priest can " do nothing for me, and I resign myself to this

" state of things. The nations stripped the priest
" of the time-honoured love they bore him, when
" the priest divested himself of one august part
" of his character, when the man of God ceased
" to be the champion of liberty.

" I am but a young man, an obscure Catholic ;
" my public life scarcely dates three months back ;
" and yet, gentlemen, I feel impelled to unbosom
" to you the secret sentiments of my soul, which
" will be a proof of my good faith only in so far
" as you recognize in them the accents of sin-
" cerity. . . . .

" I was very young, my soul had forsaken God,
" and liberty my country. My soul had forsaken
" God because I was born in the wild and stormy
" morning of this nineteenth century : liberty had
" forsaken my country, because after great mis-
" fortunes, God had given France a man greater
" even than these misfortunes themselves.

" I was still young ; I saw this capital, where
" curiosity, fancy, and a thirst for knowledge led
" me to believe the secrets of the world would be
" laid open to me. Its weight crushed me; I be-
" came a believer; once a believer I became a

" priest. Allow me to rejoice at it, gentlemen;
" for I never better understood the meaning of
" liberty than the day upon which I received, with
" the sacred unction, the right to speak of God.

" The universe opened out before me, and I
" saw that there was in man something inalienable,
" divine, eternally free: speech! The right of
" teaching was entrusted to me. I was told to
" preach the word of God even to the extremities
" of the earth ; and no one had the right to close
" my lips a single day of my life. I left the
" temple with these great destinies, and upon the
" threshold I was met by laws and servitude.....

" If I have preached disobedience to the laws,
" I have been guilty of a great fault, for laws
" are sacred. They are, next to God, the salva-
" tion of nations, and no one ought to respect them
" more than the priest, whose mission it is to teach
" nations whence comes their life, whence their
" death. Still, I confess, I do not feel for the
" laws of my country that celebrated love which
" the ancients bore theirs. When Leonidas died,
" his epitaph was this : *Passer-by, go and tell*
" *' Sparta that we died in obedience to her sacred*

"'*laws.*' I should be unwilling, gentlemen, to
" have this inscription written upon my grave : I
" should be very loath to die for the sacred laws
" of my country. For the time is gone by when
" law was the venerable channel of the traditions,
" the manners, and the worship of peoples : every-
" thing is changed. A thousand epochs, a thousand
" opinions, a thousand tyrannies ; the sword and
" the axe clash in our confused legislation ; and
" to die for such laws, would be to adore at the
" same time glory and infamy. There is one which
" I respect, which I love, by which I will stand :
" it is the Charta of France. Not that I cling
" exclusively to the shifting forms of represen-
" tative government, but because the Charta holds
" out freedom, and because when the world is in
" anarchy men have but one country, freedom. . . .
" I have protested against the appointment of
" bishops by the civil power, or rather by our
" oppressors, such is the term I have used ; and as
" the Attorney-General has insisted upon it at
" length, I lay stress upon it too. Our oppressors !
" The expression has hurt you. You have called
" me to account for it ; you have looked at my

"hands to see whether they were bruised by
"manacles. My hands are free, Mr. Attorney-
"General, but my hands are not myself. Myself
"is my thought, my speech, and, know it, this self
"is fettered in my country. You do not, indeed,
"bind my hands; and even did you, the matter
"would be but a trifling one. But if you do not
"tie up my hands, you shackle my thought, you
"do not allow me to teach—me, to whom it has
"been said '*Docete.*' The seal of your laws is
"upon my lips, when will it be broken? I have
"consequently called you my oppressors, and I
"dread bishops from your hand!

"I have charged the government with real
"faults. I have reproached it with them ener-
"getically, but without the slightest intention
"of exciting Catholics to hatred and contempt
"of it. Believe me, gentlemen, from the bosom
"of Providence, whither faith is ever directing
"our thoughts, we look upon the rise and fall of
"empires with thoughts purer than those which
"animate the men who in the greatest catastrophes
"see nothing but the conflict of human interests.
"The liberty of the Church and of the world

" appears to us to be the term of the secret judg-
" ments of God, and in this light we look upon the
" events which have changed the face of France.
" If they contribute to the freedom of the human
" conscience, they shall have a share in our love ;
" if they be untrue to their end, they cannot
" exact from us oaths of perpetual fealty, which
" are due only to our country, liberty, and God
" —three things which do not die. . . . .
" My duty is accomplished. Yours, gentlemen
" of the jury, is to acquit me of this charge.
" It is not for myself that I ask for this ac-
" quittal. There are only two things which im-
" part genius, God and a dungeon. I ought not
" then to fear one more than the other. But I
" ask you for my acquittal as an advance towards
" the alliance between faith and liberty ; as a
" token of peace and reconciliation. The Catholic
" clergy have done their duty ; they have cried
" out in terms of love to their fellow-citizens :
" the answer remains with you. I ask you for
" it again, in order that those despot underlings,
" the offshoot of the Napoleonic empire, may
" learn in their distant provinces that justice is

" meted out in France to Catholics, and that they
" are no longer to be sacrificed to worn-out pre-
" judices, and the bickerings of bygone days.

" I ask you then, gentlemen, to acquit John-
" Baptist Henry Lacordaire ; seeing that he has
" not broken the law : that he has behaved him-
" self like a good citizen, that he has defended
" his God and his liberty, and intends so to do
" until his last breath."

The two defendants were acquitted. The verdict was not given until midnight. A numerous
crowd surrounded and cheered the victors of the
day.

When the crowd had broken up, we both
returned alone in the darkness, along the quays
of the Seine. In taking leave of him, I hailed in
him the future orator. He was neither intoxicated
nor overcome by his triumph. I saw that the
little vanity consequent upon success was less
than nothing to him ; nothing but dust in the
night. But I saw him eager to instil into other
souls the spirit of devotedness and courage, and
charmed by those mutual pledges of faithfulness
and disinterested tenderness which, in young Chris-

tian hearts, shine with a lustre purer and more attractive than that of the greatest victories.

So unexpected a victory was not calculated to damp our courage. A new campaign was undertaken. We resolved to direct our chief effort upon the question of liberty of teaching. This question, already mooted under the Restoration, had been mentioned in the Charta of 1830, which in its last article promised that, *"within "the shortest possible time*, public instruction and " liberty of teaching should be granted." Government did not evince the slightest haste to carry out this decree; and the administration of the University,* by its roughness in the execution of the imperial decrees, which had created their monopoly, added to the anger and impatience of the Catholic body.

---

* In former days there were several Universities in France, like those still existing in England or Germany. But since the reign of Napoleon I., *The University* is the name given to a body of government officials who are at the head of all public schools, and were also (till the new law of M. de Falloux passed during the republic in 1850) the sole dispensers of private education.

The rector (chief government inspector) of Lyons went so far as to order the parish-priests of that town to send away the choristers, to whom they gave gratuitous instruction. On the receipt of this news, the editors of the *Avenir*, who had formed themselves into an "*agency* "*for the defence of religious liberty*," announced publicly that, "seeing that liberty must be taken, "but will not be given," three of them would open a free-school. "The University," said they, "is persecuting freedom of instruction even down "to the choristers of our churches : Well! we will "put it face to face with men." The school was opened on the 7th of May, 1831, notice having been previously given to the prefect of police.

The Abbé Lacordaire made a short and energetic speech at the opening. We taught each of us a little class of twenty children.

Two days afterwards a commissary came and ordered us to quit ; he first of all began with the children, saying, "*In the name of the law, I* "*summon you to leave.*" The Abbé Lacordaire immediately said, "*In the name of your parents,* "*whose authority I hold, I order you to stay.*"

The children cried out, " *We will stay!* " Upon
which, the police forced both children and masters
to leave, with the exception of Lacordaire, who
urged that the school rented by him was his
dwelling, and that he would pass the night there,
unless he was taken away by force.

" You go, and leave me," he said, seating
himself upon a bed with which he had provided
himself, " I will remain here alone with the law
" and my rights."

He only yielded to the touch of the police.
After this, the doors were sealed up, and an
action was immediately begun against the schoolmaster. As, whilst the different details of the
prosecution were going forward, I succeeded to
the hereditary peerage by the premature death
of my father,* and the action against us both was

----

* Nark René, Count de Montalembert, died on June 21st,
1831, and was succeeded by his eldest son, Charles, Count de
Montalembert, the author of this memoir. The dignity of a
peer having ceased to be hereditary, by a law voted in 1832,
M. de Montalembert was almost the last and the youngest peer
admitted to the House by hereditary right. Any peer prose-

indivisible, we had both to appear before the House of Peers. The case was heard on the 15th of September, and we were each condemned to a fine of one hundred francs. Such was the first act of the great suit, which was only to be gained twenty years later. It was a small price to pay for the honour and advantage of having forced upon the attention of the public a question involving the life and death of our cause, and having obliged Catholics to recognize the only ground upon which they could one day hope to conquer.

The Abbé Lacordaire achieved that day a second triumph. He understood well the difference between men and things. Hot and bold before the jury, he showed himself politic and moderate, without being less eloquent or less bold, in presence of the ninety-four peers of France, who represented so much civil and military distinction, but, at the same time, such different

---

cuted for a crime or misdemeanour could only be judged by the House of Peers.—[*Translator's Note.*]

views, and so much downfallen power. May I
be allowed to quote him again ? I hope so : for
it seems to me that no one will be tired of listening to the first accents of a voice predestined
to so glorious and sovereign an ascendant.

His opening immediately won the attention
of his audience.

" My Lords,—I look around me, and I am
" astonished. I am astonished at seeing myself
" at the bar in quality of defendant, whilst the
'" Solicitor-General* is on the ministry bench : I
" am astounded that the Solicitor-General should
" have ventured to conduct the prosecution,—he
" who is guilty of the same offence as myself,
" and who has committed it in the very house
" in which he accuses me : in your presence, and
" but so lately. For with what does he charge
" me ? With having used a right written in the
" Charta, and not yet fixed by a law ; and he
" himself asked you but lately for the head of

---

* M. Persil, since Keeper of the Seals to King Louis
Philippe, and to-day Privy-Councillor to Napoleon III.

" four ministers in virtue of a right written in
" the Charta, and not yet determined by a law.*
" If he had a right to do as he did, I too had
" a right to act as I did, with this difference,
" that he asked you for blood, whilst I attempted
" simply to give gratuitous instruction to the
" children of the poor.

" We have both acted in virtue of the 69th
" article of the Charta. If the Solicitor-General
" be guilty, how dares he accuse me? If he
" be innocent, again I ask, how dares he accuse
" me?

" I have other reasons for astonishment, my
" lords ; for the guard of honor at your doors
" has, like myself, and in the same way, violated
" the existing laws. Long before the National

---

* Prince de Polignac, MM. de Peyronnet, de Chantelauze,
and Guernon Ranville, four of King Charles X.'s ministers,
who had advised and countersigned the ordinances of July
1830, by which the Charta had been violated. They had been
tried and condemned to a lengthened imprisonment by the
House of Peers, although the law relating to ministerial
responsibility, promised by the Charta, had not yet been
drawn up.—[*Translator's Note.*]

" Guard had been organized in the manner pro-
" mised by the Charta, and whilst the act which
" disbanded it was still in vigor, it reformed, chose
" its officers, appeared in arms, not upon one
" single point, but throughout the length and
" breadth of France.

" How am I guilty if it is innocent ?

" How does it happen that wherever I look
" I see accomplices, and yet that only I and my
" friends are at the bar of the accused ?   The
" head of ministers was asked for in virtue of
" a principle of liberty not fixed by a law ; and
" when we, in virtue too of a principle of liberty
" not fixed by a law, but written in the same
" page, and in the same article of the Charta,
" attempt to bring together a few children belong-
" ing to poor families, in order to give them the
" elements of divine and human learning, we are
" proceeded against as disturbers of the public
" peace ; our children are scattered, my dwelling
" violated, and my door still sealed up.

" In all that the Solicitor-General has said,
" I have seen nothing which explains the reason
" of so much impunity in the one case, and so

" much rigor in the other, except it be, that that
" impunity was injustice, and that this rigor be
" persecution.

" If so, I understand both ; and after perse-
" cution, my lords, I make bold to ask for justice.
" . . . ."

The following is a fragment of his discussion :—

" . . . . Starting from this point,
" my lords, I cannot find words to express my
" astonishment at the *sang-froid* with which the
" Solicitor-General said to you, ' The decree of
" ' 1811* has been carried out, consequently it has
" ' force of law.' But was it carried out freely ?
" Was it carried out with the common consent ?
" Was it carried out in such a manner as to be a
" liberty for France ?

" What a mockery, my lords ! And the Soli-
" citor-General begged you, with a species of
" complacency, to remark that the decree was exe-

---

* A decree published by Napoleon I., without any of the
legal forms nominally prescribed by the Imperial Constitution.

" cuted under the empire. Since then, he has
" been kind enough to take upon himself my
" part, I must be content to repeat after him.
" It was under the empire ; it was at a time when
" France consented to nothing, since nothing was
" submitted to her decision ; it was at a time
" when those of the republicans who had escaped
" the scaffold adored on their knees the imperial
" idol; it was at a time when there were but
" two things abroad in France, glory and silence.

" But was this slavery sufficiently long to
" allow it to be said that it had acquired the
" power and majesty given by time ?

" Count the days, my lords, and thank Pro-
" vidence who shortened them. Between the 15th
" of November, 1811, and the 1st of April, 1814,
" between the decree which protected the univer-
" sity by arbitrary penalties, and the act which
" hurled Napoleon from the throne, there inter-
" vened two years, three months, and six days.
" Is this a sufficient space to cover slavery with
" the veil which time throws over everything ?

" The decree of 1811 was enforced as law
" under the empire : you have yourself said so,

" Mr. Solicitor-General ; you have yourself laid
" this down as the strongest point of your argu-
" ment, and you observed to the Court, with a
" tinge of pride, that under the empire no one
" had been found bold enough to withstand the
" will of Napoleon.

" I willingly consent to treat the case upon this
" ground, and I am anxious to repeat the proof
" by which you endeavour to show that the decree
" of 1811 had force of law under the imperial
" sceptre. You tell me that it is because it was
" executed. Now, where the sword commands,
" obedience is prompt, and if no other condition
" be requisite to render the will of man law, vio-
" lence is the supreme lawgiver of the human
" race,—a fact becomes a right, and the silence
" of terror the voice of God.

" If other conditions be requisite, what are
" they ? Have they been fulfilled in the case of
" the decree of 1811 ? The Solicitor-General has
" left this matter completely untouched. He con-
" fined himself to the haughty remark, 'The
" 'decree has been executed ;' intentionally add-
" ing, that it was under the empire. Under the

" empire forsooth! There was of course at that
" time such an amount of liberty and civil courage
" in France, that the execution of the imperial
" will necessarily gave it the force of law ; that is
" to say, stamped it with the consent of the
" nation or its representatives; in other words,
" lent it the character of justice! No, if the
" doctrine of the ministry were true; if it were
" possible that in France the simple execution of
" a decree could make that decree law, we should
" have to fly our country, and seek in the lowest
" scale of civilization for a little of that liberty
" which is never totally lost, unless it be among
" nations by whom the word violence is received
" as a synonyme for something sacred, and with
" whom the orders of the master are law, pro-
" vided the slave has answered : I obey."

After having so well spoken of the Napoleonian
empire before so many old servants of the imperial
power, he thus concludes :

" Had time not been wanting to me I should
" have made every possible concession the prose-
" cution could have desired, and even upon the
" assumption that we were guilty of the violation

" of a decree sanctioned by penalties, I should
" have drawn from our very guilt the proof of
" our innocence. For, my lords, there are righteous
" faults, and the violation of one law may some-
" times be the fulfilment of a higher. In the
" first law-suit on freedom of education, in that
" memorable trial in which Socrates succumbed,
" he was evidently in fault against the gods, and
" consequently against the laws of his country.

   " Still pagan as well as Christian posterity
" have branded his judges and accusers; they
" have acquitted none but the criminal and the
" executioner; the criminal because he disobeyed
" the laws of Athens to obey higher ones; the
" executioner because he wept whilst handing the
" cup to the condemned.

   " And I, my lords, would have proved to you,
" that in disregarding this decree of the empire
" I have merited well of the laws of my country,
" served her liberty well, as also the cause and
" the future of all Christian peoples. Time will
" not allow me to dwell upon this thought: I
" am satisfied since it leaves me your justice.
" Enough! When Socrates, in the first great

E

" struggle for freedom of instruction, was pre-
" paring to leave his judges, he said to them :
" ' We are going out—you to live, I to die.'   It
" will not be thus, my lords, that we shall leave
" you.   Whatever be your verdict, we shall go
" out to live : for liberty and religion are im-
" mortal, and the sentiments of a pure heart
" which you have heard upon our lips are alike
" imperishable." *

Death has not spared more than four or five
of the noble peers who were thus addressed ; but
those who still remain will not gainsay me when I
state that the whole house, which, with its respect
for the unlimited liberty of the defence, had coldly
and patiently listened to the other speakers, was
charmed by the eloquence and person of the
young orator.

The happy boldness of his improvisation had
aroused the attention of the least well-disposed.
This proud language, which to-day perhaps may

-----

* *Moniteur*, September 20th, 1831.

appear extravagant to many of my readers, did
not shock the noble assembly in which sat so
many illustrious personages ; and when, a little
later, my age entitled me to take my seat among
those who had been our judges,* I found still
living the memory of the priest, who, during the
cruel storms of 1831, had for a moment captivated
them by his enchanting eloquence.

I shall be excused for having spoken at such
length of the events of this memorable year.
There is no one, however obscure and useless his
life, who, at its decline, does not feel himself
irresistibly carried back to the time when the first
fires of enthusiasm were kindled in his soul and
on his lips: no one who does not inhale, with a
kind of ecstasy, the fragrance of these memories,
and who is not tempted to an innocent exaggeration of their charm and their splendour.

"Days happy and sorrowful," said he ; "days

---

* According to the Charta, no peer could sit in the House
until he was twenty-five years old.

" spent in labour and enthusiasm ; days such as
" are seen once in a lifetime !"

I am not fearful of exaggerating the real value
of these struggles, which, as far as the substance
of the points in question go, ended in victory, and
determined the attitude of Catholics in France
and elsewhere, from the revolution of July until
the second empire. The present generation can
form no idea of the strong and generous passions
which at that time mastered all hearts. There
were many less newspapers, and many less readers
than to-day. (The subscribers to the *Avenir* never
amounted to three thousand.) Postal and other
communications were much more difficult ; there
were neither railroads nor electric telegraphs, and
in our journeys of propagandism we took three
days and three nights to travel from Paris to
Lyons, in wretched stage-coaches.

But what life in souls ! what ardour of mind !
what disinterested love of one's flag ! of one's
cause ! what deep impressions stamped upon the
mind of youth at that time by an idea, a piece
of devotedness, a great example, an act of faith
or courage !

He who has taken his place among the first of our living poets, our illustrious and dear colleague, whom the French Academy called into its ranks, as a worthy precursor of Lacordaire, has described, in memorable lines, the worth of that youth to which he belonged.*

In order to form an idea of the pure and unselfish enthusiasm then alive among the young

---

* M. de Laprade.
" Ah! j'ai connu des jours et je les ai vécu
" Où les droits désarmés, où l'idéal vaincu,
" Le penseur qu'on proscrit et le Dieu qu'on délaisse,
" Avaient au moins pour eux les cœurs de la jeunesse !...
" Sous ses drapeaux la Muse enrôla de tout temps
" Le bataillon sacré des âmes de vingt ans...
" Alors aux grandes voix les cœurs étaient ouverts...
" Tous, alors, adoptant nos poëtes pour guides,
" Nous montions, dédaigneux des intérêts sordides,
" Fiers, altérés du beau plutôt que du bonheur,
" Amoureux de l'amour, du droit, du vieil honneur,
" Et tous prêts à mourir, purs de toute autre envie,
" Pour ces biens qui font seuls les causes de la vie...
" Ecoliers, jeunes fous, c'étaient là nos orgies,
" L'ivresse où nous puisions nos rudes élégies ;
" C'était notre soleil dans les travaux obscurs
" Qui nous ont gardés fiers en nous conservant purs."

clergy, and a certain number of honest and noble young laymen, one must have lived in those days, read in their eyes, listened to their secrets, grasped their quivering hands, formed, in the heat of the fight, bonds which death alone could sever ; one must above all, read the speeches and private correspondence of Lacordaire, who wrote, two months after his appearance at the House of Peers: "However cruel time be, he will never blight the "charms of the year which has just closed ; that "year will be eternally to my heart like a virgin "just expired."

It was already waning, that year which had rolled by like one of those holy and glorious days whose very twilight is full of radiance and joy.

The checkered career of the *Avenir* was drawing to a close. The ardent and generous sympathy called forth by it was more than counterbalanced by the violent repugnance evinced towards it both by the partisans of democratic absolutism, and the tried friends of monarchical authority. The ever growing distrust of the episcopacy was a much more serious obstacle. To new and fair practical notions, honest in themselves, which have for the last twenty years been the daily bread of Catholic polemics, we had been foolish enough to add extreme and rash theories ; and to defend both with that absolute logic which loses, even when it does not dishonour, every cause.

The giving up of the pecuniary indemnity stipulated for the clergy by the Concordat between Pius VII. and Napoleon, was one of the vagaries of this logic, precisely similar to that which to-day urges certain men to cry for the abolition of the Pope's temporal power, out of love for his personal freedom.

Our task was further compromised in the eyes of the clergy, on the one hand, by M. de la Mennais' philosophical system on certitude, which he pretended to make the basis of his politics as well as of his theology ; and on the other by the excessive ultramontanism of that great writer, and his first disciples ; for it is well to add, for the information of those who have not sounded the depths of French fickleness, that at that time, ultramontane ideas were quite as unpopular with the large majority of the clergy as gallicanism is to-day.

Finally our material resources, exhausted not only by a daily paper, but by so many different law suits and publications, ran short.

We were consequently condemned to silence, at least for a time. But at the same time that we announced the discontinuance of the paper, (Nov. 15, 1831, thirteen months after its first appearance,) we announced the departure of its three chief editors for Rome, for the purpose of submitting to the Sovereign Pontiff the questions debated between our adversaries and ourselves; promising beforehand absolute submission to the papal decision. This idea originated, I believe, with Lacordaire. I find it put forward in the article of his, for which he had been prosecuted a year previously, and which ended thus:

"We commend our protest to all Frenchmen "in whom faith and shame are not dead : to our "brothers of the United States, of Ireland, and "Belgium ; to all those who are struggling for the "liberty of the world, wherever they may be. "We will, if need be, carry that protest to the "city of the apostles, to the steps of the Con- "fession of St. Peter, and we shall see who will

" dare to stand in the way of the Pilgrims of God " and of liberty."*

No one evinced the least desire to stop them; and it was really a pity, for this journey was a mistake. To force Rome to pronounce upon questions which she had allowed to be discussed freely for more than a year, was, to say the least, a singular pretension.

To be other than infinitely grateful to her for her silence was to mistake all the exigencies and all the advantages of our position.

Such a mistake can be accounted for in young men without any experience of the things of the world, and of the Church ; but how account for it, and above all excuse it in an illustrious priest, already formed by age, as was the Abbé de la Mennais, who was at that time over fifty, and who had already lived in Rome, where Leo XII. had received him with great marks of distinction ?

From the moment of our arrival at Rome, the

---

* *Avenir*, Nov. 25, 1830.

cautious reception everywhere given us, showed us plainly that we should not get the answer we were expecting. After having been asked for an explanatory memorial, which was drawn up by Lacordaire, we remained two months without hearing anything. Then Cardinal Pacca wrote to M. de la Mennais, that the Pope, whilst mindful of his services and his good intentions, had been pained to see us moot questions and put forth opinions at least dangerous; that he would submit our doctrines to examination, and that as this examination might be long, we could return to our country. Pope Gregory XVI. then consented to receive us; he treated us with that kind familiarity which was natural to him; he did not reprove us in the slightest; but he did not allude even remotely to the business which had brought us to Rome.

The solution was certainly anything but brilliant and flattering, but it was undoubtedly the most favourable we had a right to expect.

Lacordaire was quite prepared for it. He rightly looked upon it as nothing but a paternal warning, the most delicate imaginable, one that left the least trace—which decided nothing and compromised no one. During this residence of two months and a half in the Eternal City, a great peace and light had risen upon his soul.

I see him still, wandering the live-long day among ruins and monuments, stopping as though lost in admiration (with that keen sentiment of true beauty which never failed him) at all the sublime and unique sites which Rome offers; charmed above all by the soft and incomparable beauty of her horizons—then returning to our common home, to inculcate upon M. de la Mennais, reserve, resignation, submission—in a word, good sense.

The shortcomings and weaknesses of everything human which comes in contact with divine things did not escape him, but they appeared to him merged in the mysterious splendour of tradition and authority. He, the journalist, the *Bourgeois* of 1830, the liberal democrat, had taken in at first sight not only the inviolable majesty of the Supreme Pontificate, but its difficulties, its far-seeing and patient designs, its gentleness in dealing with men and the things of this world. The faith of the Catholic priest had in that noble heart immediately dispelled all the fumes of pride, had vanquished all the seductions, all the waywardness of talent, all the intoxication of conflict. With the penetration which accompanies faith and humility, he pronounced upon our pretensions the verdict since borne out by time, that great auxiliary of the Church and of truth. It was then, I make bold to believe, that God marked him for ever with the seal of his grace, and assured to him the reward due to the unconquerable fidelity of a truly priestly soul.

In the meantime the great writer, who had been called in the tribune *the last of the Fathers of the Church*, the eloquent and renowned doctor, the aged priest crowned for the last twenty years by the admiration and confidence of the Catholic world, was struggling with all his might against good sense and evidence, as well as against his duty as a Catholic and a priest. The youth had understood all ; the formed man, the man of genius, wanted to ignore everything. Prudence, clearsightedness, dignity, and good faith, were all on the side of the disciple, and they became in his mouth so many solemn and pathetic *warnings* addressed to his cherished master. Vain and powerless attempt! Far from listening to the tender and respectful, but withal firm and honest voice of his young follower, the master foolishly gave way to his temper, and daily broke away further from his antecedents, from everything which ought to have restrained and enlightened him. He listened to none but two or three covert enemies of the pontifical authority; he was already meditating the unnatural alliances which lost him. Faith began to make way for sorry fancies in his soul. After Cardinal Pacca's letter, and the papal audience, Lacordaire resolutely put the following dilemma to him : " Either we ought not to have " come, or we must submit and keep silence." M. de la Mennais would not agree to this, and answered : " I will push matters, and urge for an immediate " decision, I will wait at Rome, and then make up " my mind." The real priest then took his determination : without overstepping the bounds of the most respectful deference, and distracted, as he himself told me, " by the agonies of conscience

" battling against genius," he announced his resolution of returning to France, and awaiting
there in silence, without remaining inactive, the
decision of authority :—" Next to speech," he
said, " silence is the greatest power in the
" world."

M. de la Mennais, who knew how to be, at
times, the most fond and paternal of men, was
never tender towards Lacordaire ; he saw him
leave Rome without regret, rid, as he supposed,
of a troublesome censor, and an unfaithful disciple. Before, as well as after, his departure,
this faithful friend made the most persevering
efforts to deliver me as he had himself. Scarcely
had he returned to France when he wrote to me :
" There is no spiritual disunion between us ; my
" whole life through I will defend liberty ; even
" before M. de la Mennais had uttered a word
" in her favor, she was the object of my thoughts,
" and my very life. If he carries out his plan,
" remember that all his oldest friends and his
" most attached colleagues will abandon him, and
" that, driven by the false liberals into a course
" in which success is out of the question, there

" is no language sad enough to tell what will
" happen. . . . .*

" Let us not yoke our ideas and our hearts
" together : for the ideas of man, like the clouds
" which flit across the sun, are bright and fugitive
" like them."

I remained deaf to his voice. He pitied and
excused me. " You are younger than I am, and,
" consequently, you are more often mistaken."
And still at this very time, he was marking out
the path of truth to the Abbé de la Mennais,
who was nearly double his age.

The sequel is well known. M. de la Mennais, after waiting four months, blind to the fact
that this long delay was, at the same time, the
safeguard of his honor and his future, lost patience, and left Rome, publicly announcing his
intention of returning to France, in order to continue, without any further formality, the *Avenir*.

Upon hearing this, Lacordaire determined to

————————

* 22nd April, 1832.

go into Germany, and spend some time there in studious seclusion.

We, too, took in Germany on our way back to France. Providence threw all three of us together at Munich, where we were overtaken by the famous encyclical letter of the 15th of August, 1832, which had been directly evoked by the last threats of the Abbé de la Mennais, and in which, although he was not named, his new doctrines were, for the most part, manifestly condemned.

CHAPTER III.

RUPTURE WITH M. DE LA MENNAIS.

OUR submission was immediate and unreserved.
It was immediately published, and we returned to
Paris "victorious over ourselves," according to
the expression of him who had so well foreseen,
and so nobly accepted defeat. He added with
Montaigne, "There are defeats more glorious than
" victory."

Lacordaire, who believed in the good faith
of M. de la Mennais, was desirous of accompanying him into Brittany, to live with him in the
solitude of La Chesnaie, and prepare himself in
retreat for whatever mission God might assign
him by his Church, and through future events.

F

Amid this wild and melancholy scenery, he soon discovered the mistake he had made in believing that the Abbé de la Mennais was resigned to his defeat, and would turn it to the service of the Church, and his own glory. He daily saw the gulf widen which lay between their judgments upon the past, and their ideas concerning the future. La Mennais was gnawing his bond, his heart was ulcerated by dark resentment; he was brooding over a general war, a rapid and universal catastrophe which should put everything into its proper place, and himself into his. The frequentation of each other's society became impossible by their perpetual disagreement upon matters which embraced, in their consequences, the whole of the present, as well as the future. Finally, unable, as at Rome, to bear this state of things, Lacordaire burst, for the second and last time, the bond which yoked him to this great and unfortunate man, whose ruin he foresaw, and was unwilling to share.

On the 11th of December, 1832, he left, after having written to M. de la Mennais the following letter :—

" I shall leave La Chesnaie this evening. Honor
" obliges me so to do, since I am convinced that;
" for the future, my life would be useless to you,
" on account of the divergence of our opinions
" touching the Church and society : which diver-
" gence has but daily increased, notwithstanding
" my earnest endeavours to follow the develop-
" ment of your opinions. I believe that, neither
" during my life, nor even long after, will repub-
" lican institutions be possible in France, or in
" any other country of Europe, and I cannot adopt
" any system grounded upon an opposite view.
" Without giving up my liberal ideas, I see and
" believe that the Church has had grave reasons,
" in the profound corruption of parties, for re-
" fusing to hurry matters according to our wishes.
" I respect her views and my own. Your opinions
" may be more exact, more profound, than mine,
" and, seeing your natural superiority over me,
" I ought to be satisfied that such is the case;
" but man is not made up of reason alone; and
" not being able to rid myself of the ideas which
" divide us, it is but right that I should put an
" end to a community of life, which is a great

" advantage to me, and a burthen to you. Con-
" science, no less than honor, obliges me to do so,
" for I must employ my life somehow or other
" in God's service; and not being able to follow
" you, what should I be doing here but wearying
" and discouraging you, shackling your plans, and
" sacrificing myself to no purpose?

" You will never know but in heaven the suf-
" fering I have undergone for the last year, from
" the simple fear of giving you pain. In all my
" doubts, in all my perplexities, I have had you
" alone in view; and however bitter may one day
" be my existence, nothing will ever equal the
" grief which I feel on the present occasion. I
" leave you in peace with the Church, higher than
" ever in public opinion, so superior to your
" enemies, that they are as nothing. I could
" choose no better time to do that which, while
" giving you some pain, will, believe me, spare
" you much greater. I do not exactly know as
" yet what I shall do, whether I shall go to the
" United States, or remain in France, and in what
" position. Wherever I may be, you will ever
" have proofs of the respect and attachment for

" you which I shall ever cherish,—and I beg of
" you to accept this expression of them from a
" broken heart."

This separation was but the prelude to those
which ended by leaving M. de la Mennais without
a single one of the disciples whom his genius and
renown had fascinated ; and yet it was at first
neither understood nor approved. Lacordaire
suffered from the unfairness of several of his
warmest admirers, even from that of his best
friend, with single-minded resignation and clear-
sighted confidence in the future. We shall see in
a letter written by him at that time the honest,
elevated ideas which alone guided him :—" I feel
" as deeply as any one," he wrote, " the respect
" due to souvenirs, and even supposing M. de
" la Mennais fell away from the Church, and
" became the most noxious heresiarch that ever
" existed, there would still be an infinite distance
" between his enemies and me ; and no one would
" read what I might be obliged to write without
" feeling at once the painfulness of my position,
" the lasting character of my respect, the disin-
" terestedness and faithfulness of my conscience.

" The great moments of a man's life are those
" in which he is struggling with contradictory
" circumstances, with great conflicting duties.
" It will be known in heaven whether or not I
" have acted with the inconsiderateness of one
" who breaks without reason the engagements he
" has contracted."*

The position taken up by the young priest
who, at thirty years of age, had evinced such
consummate prudence, was but too quickly justified. M. de la Mennais has, in his *Affaires de
Rome*, traced with his own hand the lamentable
story of those three years, during which, the
zealot of the absolute and universal infallibility
of the Pope passed through an unheard of series
of quibbles and retractations, feigned submissions,
and contradictory declarations, until at last he
openly revolted against the simplest and most
lawful exercise of that pontifical authority which
he himself had forced to pronounce upon cer-

---

* 19th August, 1833.

tain moral and theological questions. Lacordaire looked on with sorrow but calmness, following link by link the chain which was unravelling itself. Very reserved in public, he frequently confided his private impressions to the sharers of his intimacy. " M. de la Mennais," said he, after one of these strange freaks of that already lost genius, " declares that *'for many reasons,* " *' and chiefly because it is the province of the* " *' Holy See to decide what is good and useful* " *' for the Church, he is resolved to stand aloof* " *' from all matters touching her.'* I have to " remark that nothing can be more anti-Catholic " than this saying . . . . Were this the case, " the Church would be unfortunate indeed. Her " children have never any right, under whatever " pretext, to stand aloof from what concerns her : " they must act according to their position and " capacity, as M. de la Mennais has done up to the " present ; but their action must be accompanied " by submission to the direction of the Holy See ; " they are not to be their own guides . . . . " No amount of talent, no services however great, " compensate for the harm done to the Church by

" a separation, of whatever nature, or by an
" action done without her bosom. I would rather
" throw myself into the sea with a millstone
" round my neck, than entertain hopes, ideas, or
" support even good works outside the Church." *

A little later on, after a new episode in the
conflict between the Papacy and its ancient champion, he said, " M. de la Mennais' misfortune
" does not so much lie in his haughty character,
" in his very imperfect knowledge of human and
" divine things, as in his contempt of the ponti-
" fical authority, and of the painful situation of
" the Holy See. He has blasphemed Rome in her
" misfortunes : it is the crime of Cham, the crime
" which has, next to deicide, been visited on
" earth with the most palpable and lasting pun-
" ishment. Woe to him who troubles the Church!
" Woe to him who blasphemes the Apostles !
" The lot of the Church is to be victorious still ;
" the time of Antichrist is not yet come. M. de

---

* October 6th, 1833.

" la Mennais' fall will not check the formidable
" march of truth: this very fall will but serve
" it.* . . . . . .

" I am accused of being merciless towards
" him! Ah! if ever I had discovered in the
" Abbé de la Mennais a single real yearning, a
" single sentiment of humility, that interesting
" something which misfortune lends its victim,
" I should have been unable to see it and think
" of it without being moved to the inmost depths
" of my soul!

" When we were together, and I fancied I
" discovered in him resignation, sentiments de-
" void of pride and passion, I cannot express
" what I felt. But these moments were few
" indeed, and all that I can call to mind is
" stamped with a character of wilfulness and
" blindness such as dries up pity. You I pity,
" because you are suffering through the fault
" of another, because, although there are in you

---

* 2nd December, 1833.

" many personal illusions and faults which God
" will one day lay to your charge, still you are
" a victim ; a victim of the goodness of your
" heart. But he ! well, since my friend is so
" unjust towards me, I must expect justice from
" God alone. He will bear witness to the purity
" of my intentions; He will say why I sided with
" the Church against a man ; He will show on
" which side was single-minded faith, candour,
" and consistency ; He will show who was, of all,
" the real friend of the Abbé de la Mennais, and
" whose was the advice which, if followed, would
" have raised his glory and virtue higher than
" ever.

" The hour of justice will, I feel convinced,
" come round sooner than is imagined ; but if
" it does not come in this world, I shall not find
" fault with Providence. The accomplishment of
" my duty amply satisfies me." *

This hour did, in fact, soon come. Three

---

* 3rd February, 1834.

months after these lines were penned, M. de la
Mennais put an end to all the doubts which might
have been left by his acts and protestations, by
the publication of his *Paroles d'un Croyant.*

Lacordaire considered himself obliged to answer this demonstration by *Considérations sur le
Système Philosophique de M. de la Mennais,* for
to this system he attributed all the errors of the
master.

I cannot imagine why this publication had
neither the vogue nor the success it so well
deserved, since it contains some of the finest
pages produced by his pen ; for instance, the following one which ends it. " Truth is not always
" powerful enough to maintain the equilibrium of
" forces ; otherwise error would never triumph
" over truth. There exists then, in this world,
" a necessity for a power capable of protecting
" weak against strong minds, and of freeing them
" from the most terrible bondage of all—that of
" the mind.

" This power came to my aid ; it was not I
" who freed myself, it was this power. Arrived
" at Rome, at the shrine of the holy Apostles

" Peter and Paul, I cast myself upon my knees,
" and said to God: 'Lord, I begin to feel my
" 'weakness, my sight is growing dim, I am
" 'unable to discern error from truth: have pity
" 'on thy servant who comes to Thee in the sin-
" 'cerity of his heart, listen to the prayer of the
" 'poor.'

" I remember neither the day nor the hour,
" but I remember that I saw what I had not
" hitherto seen; I left Rome free and victorious.
" I learnt from my own experience that the
" Church is the deliverer of the human mind;
" and as every other liberty has its source in that
" of the human mind, I saw in their true light
" the questions which to-day divide the world.

" Yes, the world is seeking for peace and
" liberty, but it is seeking them along the high-
" road to grief and slavery. The Church alone
" gave them to the human race, and alone, in her
" bosom, outraged by her children, she preserves
" their sacred and inexhaustible fountain. When
" nations shall be weary of parricide, they will
" there find the good which they have lost. This
" is the reason why the priest will not take part

" in the bloody and unfruitful broils of his age;
" he will pray for the present and the future.
" . . . . He will tell the present generation
" that outside truth neither peace nor liberty are
" possible. . . . . He will thank God that
" he lives at a time when ambition is out of the
" question; he will understand that the greater
" the agitation of mankind, the more mighty is
" the peace which reigns upon the brow and in
" the soul of the priest; that the deeper men
" plunge into anarchy, the mightier is the unity
" of the Church; that the more powerful men are
" in appearance, the mightier is the external weak-
" ness of the Church, who lives by the power of
" God alone; that the more the world prophesies
" the death of Christianity, the more glorious will
" Christianity one day be, when time, faithful to
" eternity, shall have swept away that proud dust
" which does not seem to imagine, that in order to
" be something in the future, it is necessary to be
" something in the present, and that nothing gives
" nothing. In fine, the priest will be what the
" Church is—peaceful, charitable, patient;—a pil-
" grim who scatters blessings around him on his

" way, and who is not surprised at being mis-
" understood by the world, since he is not of it.

" O Rome! thus didst thou appear to me.
" Seated amidst the storms of Europe, thou
" betrayedst no fear for thyself, no weakness ;
" thy gaze, bent upon the four quarters of the
" world, followed with sublime clear-sightedness
" the unravelling of human in their connection
" with divine things : the tempest, which left
" thee calm, because the Spirit of God was with
" thee, lent thee, in the eyes of the simple faith-
" ful, less accustomed to the changes of time,
" a something which tinged his admiration with
" compassion.

" . . . . . O Rome! I did not underrate thee
" because I found no kings prostrate at thy gates :
" I kissed thy dust with unspeakable joy and
" respect : thou didst appear to me what thou
" really art, the benefactress of the human race in
" past, its hope in future ages, the only relic of
" greatness left standing to-day in Europe, the
" captive of universal jealousy, the queen of the
" world. . . . . . . O Rome! one of thy children
" to whom thou didst restore peace, wrote, on

" his return into his country, this book. He lays
" it at thy feet as a token of his gratitude, he
" submits it to thy judgment as a proof of his
" faith."

Throughout the whole of this book there was
not a single injurious or violent expression against
M. de la Mennais : it seemed as though the un-
usual restraint to which the young writer had
subjected himself, had, in certain parts, slightly
marred his style, and shackled his thought.

Some Catholic writers nevertheless blamed
publicly what they called "*an attack* of Lacordaire's upon his old master :" among others the
much regretted Baron d'Eckstein, and Father
Ventura, who ought to have bitterly regretted the
encouragement lavished by him on M. de la Mennais
during the latter portion of his stay at Rome. Lacordaire was not daunted by these imputations.
" Now," he wrote, " I have completely fulfilled
" my duty towards M. de la Mennais. I have said
" touching the school he desired to found, that
" which a ten years' personal experience has taught
" me, and had I done nothing but that in my life,
" I should die happy. My conscience is at ease,

" it breathes at last ; after ten years' suffering I
" am beginning to live. . . . . . . A few at least
" understand me ; they know that I have become
" neither a republican, a juste-milieu, nor a legi-
" timist, but that I have made one step towards
" that noble character of the priest, above all
" parties, though sympathizing with every weak-
" ness. They know that the result of my journey
" to Rome has been to soften down my ideas, to
" withdraw me from the fatal whirlwind of pole-
" mics, to attach me exclusively to the things of
" God, and through the things of God, to the slow
" progressive happiness of nations. They know
" that the only cause of my separation from a
" celebrated man, was my unwillingness to plunge
" deeper with him into those unfortunate daily
" politics, and the impossibility of getting him to
" take up the position where the applause of the
" Church awaited him, and where he would have
" done more for the emancipation of humanity
" than he will ever do upon his present ground." *

---

* 17th April, 1834.

" I am no saint, I am but too conscious of it,
" but I have within me an unselfish love of
" truth, and although I have endeavoured to ex-
." " tricate myself honorably from the abyss in which
" I was, no single thought of ambition or pride
" was ever for an instant the spring of my conduct
" on that occasion. Pride has always whispered
" to me, ' Stay where you are, do not change, do not
" 'lay yourself open to the reproaches of your old
" ' friends.' Divine grace spoke louder, ' Trample
" ' upon human respect, give glory to God and
" 'the Holy See.' My policy consisted solely
" in my honest submission. If everything has
" turned out as I foresaw, I only foresaw it by
" putting aside my own opinion. I do not rejoice
" at the abyss created by stubbornness beneath
" a man who has rendered signal service to the
" Church ; I hope God will check him in time ;
" but I do rejoice that the Sovereign Pontiff, the
" father, not of one, but of all Christians, has at
" last settled by his authority questions which
" were ruining my native Church in its very flower,
" which were leading astray a multitude of souls,
" *honestly mistaken*, of which questions I so long

" and so bitterly felt the wretched charm.   May
" my personal triumph, if such there have been,
" be forgotten, and may the Church of France,
" after this great and memorable lesson, flourish
" in the peaceful activity resulting from unity!
" May we all forgive each other the errors of
" our youth, and pray together for him who
" caused them by the superabundance of an imagi-
" nation too lovely not to be deplored."*

Unfortunately these prayers were not heard.
They went forth during twenty years from a
multitude of souls, which hoped against hope,
but in vain.   No token of reconciliation, no sign
of repentance, came to the consolation of those
who would have given a thousand lives for the
life of that soul.   No other shelter has remained
for their trust but the impenetrable immensity
of divine mercy.   Still M. de la Mennais, in
plunging deeper and deeper into the abyss, did
not drag down with him a single individual.
Unless I mistake, he is the only example in

---

* 2nd August, 1834.

the history of Christianity, of a man, who, possessed of everything that goes to the formation of the most formidable heresiarch, did not succeed in tearing away from the centre of unity, the humblest of her children.

But amongst those souls, *honestly mistaken*, and deeply shaken by the empire of that fatal genius, there was one which Lacordaire loved above all, and which, after all the others, persisted in a disinterested attachment, less perhaps to the person of the fallen apostle, than to the great idea which seemed buried in his fall. From the midst of his personal trials and struggles, Lacordaire devoted to this soul the intensest ardour of his zeal, the purest and most violent passion of his heart. It was for this soul, that, unknown to the world, he poured out the richest treasures of his eloquence ; " *Vadit ad illam quæ perierat donec inveniat eam.*" Would that I could say all, and quote the numerous letters, which, for the space of nearly three years, pursued this ungrateful task ! One day, perhaps, when all the spectators and actors of this struggle, shall, like him, have disappeared, these letters may fall into hands which will find in them wherewith to write in the history of that glorious life, a page which will not be the least touching.

I have just read them, after the lapse of so many years, with an emotion which no words can pourtray. I doubt whether his genius and his goodness ever shone more purely and more brightly than in this obscure and stubborn combat for the salvation of a well-loved soul. In the vain hope of escaping the pain and torment of a too cruel conflict I made for Germany, whither I was followed by the appeals of M. de la Mennais. Even whilst considering himself obliged as a priest to sign formularies of submission to the Holy See, the unfortunate man answered my fears and my filial representations by congratulating me on the independence of my position as a layman : he urged me to cling to it at any price. "That voice," he wrote, "which formerly " shook the world, would not to-day move a " set of little school-boys."*

---

* Letter of August 5th, 1834.

But the same post which brought me these poisoned letters, brought me others much more numerous, in which the true priest, the real friend, pleaded the cause of truth, by pointing out to me the ever accessible heights of light and peace. He even came in person to seek me out, and exhort me at the shrine of St. Elizabeth.* Before as well as after this too short journey, he returned to the charge with unflagging energy and unconquerable perseverance.

Sacrificed, misunderstood, repulsed, he nevertheless continued his fruitless warnings and his ever verified predictions; but with what logic, what keen and touching eloquence, what a charming mixture of severity and humble affection, what salutary turns of unsparing frankness and irresistible sweetness! Providence in its tenderest mercies could have done neither better nor more. After having laid down the truth in its stern and inviolable majesty, he decked it with all the

---

* At Warburg in Hessia.

images of his poetical fancy, and employing by turns entreaty and reasoning, he mingled with unanswerable arguments the cry of a heart unparalleled in its brotherly and unwearied devotedness. The following page, taken from among a hundred others of the same stamp, will give some notion of his efforts:

" The Church does not say to you :* *See.*
" This power does not belong to her.   She says to
" you : *Believe.*   She tells you, at twenty-three
" years, attached as you are to certain ideas, what
" she told you at your first communion : ' *Receive*
" ' *the hidden and incomprehensible God ; humble*
" ' *thy reason before God, and before the Church,*
" ' *His mouth-piece.*'   Why indeed has the Church
" been given us, unless to bring us back to truth,
" when we mistake error for it. . . . .   You
" are astonished at what the Holy See requires
" of M. de la Mennais. . . . .   It is un-
" doubtedly harder to submit after having spoken

---

* The second person singular is used in the French, it being a mark of tender familiarity.

" out before men, than when God alone has been
" the witness of our thoughts.

" This is the trial peculiar to great talents.
" The greatest men in the Church have had to
" break their lives into two, and in a lower order
" all conversion is exactly the same thing.

" Listen to this voice too unheeded by you, for
" who will warn you, if I do not? Who will love
" you enough to treat you without pity? Who
" will cauterize your wounds, if not he who kisses
" them with so much love, and who would suck
" the poison out of them at the peril of his life."

I was not a rebel, as might be supposed
from these ardent remonstrances, I was only
vacillating and troubled. Whilst obstinately resisting the pressing entreaties of Lacordaire, I
was doing my best to persuade M. de la Mennais
that silence and patience were his best course;
and to obtain this result, I could safely remind
him of my faithful devotedness, as I was then the
last to stand by him. But I was irritated with
my younger and dearer friend for having taken
a more public and decisive course. I rashly
reproached him with his apparent forgetfulness

of the liberal aspirations which had animated us both. When at last I yielded, it was but slowly, and as though unwillingly, and not until I had made that generous heart bleed. The struggle had been too protracted. I speak of it with confusion, with remorse, for I did not then do him all the justice he deserved. The avowal of this fault will be its expiation, and I offer this avowal as a homage to the great soul which has now found the judge it appealed to with such well-grounded confidence. Then and thus it was that I was able to cast into the very depths of that soul a look at first troubled and irritated, but since then and now bathed in the tears of undying gratitude. It is from that soul that I learned to understand and venerate the only power to bow down to, which is greatness. The prisoner of error and of pride, I was freed by him who then appeared to me the ideal of the priest, such as he has himself defined him : " Firm as a diamond, and softer than a mother."

CHAPTER IV.

HIS SOLITARY LIFE AT PARIS.——CONFERENCES OF THE
COLLEGE STANISLAS.——FIRST SERIES OF SERMONS AT
NOTRE-DAME.

BUT I hear sceptical and cynical voices inter-
rupting me. Is all that you relate there true ?
Was there then, in modern France, such as we
now see her, a time when people had this passionate and single-minded love of their flag—when
they really struggled and suffered for it—when
they leagued together, braced themselves up,
devoted themselves, and became enthusiastic com-
batants for ideas, principles,—for the simple life
of the soul—when a whole generation of priests

and Christians went out to meet the enemies of the faith with no other arms than those of confidence in their common rights and liberties, ambitioning nothing but a fair share of the heritage won back by justice and honour ?

Yes, young people, believe it ; such a time did exist. There were amongst us, in this country, and in this century, such people and such days. And you who are no longer young, you formed, or feigned to form part of them ; you swelled those ranks bewitched with eloquence and enthusiasm ; you, who to-day doubt of everything you have either forgotten or betrayed!   You looked with ecstasy upon that great monk, that great orator whom you have since deserted ; you, who would deny life because it no longer dwells in you, and who are no longer able to scan the height from which you have fallen.

Ah ! it is but too true ; that time which then to our youthful ardour appeared too cold and colourless, was totally unlike our time. To appreciate its worth, we have had to sink into that of which we are the indignant captives.

Let us, however, continue our task, and follow

the young Abbé Lacordaire in the modest and obscure life which he led on his return from Rome.

Scarcely had he returned to Paris, when the first and formidable outbreak of the cholera occurred; and with that cold calm courage which ever distinguished him, he immediately devoted himself to the sick and dying. He passed his days in a temporary hospital established at the *Greniers d'Abondance.* Ill-feeling towards the clergy was then at its height; the administration declined the assistance of the Archbishop of Paris, and priests could not show themselves in the streets in their cassocks. " There are here," he wrote to me, " neither sisters of Charity, nor " chaplain, nor ordinary clergy. My presence, " and that of two other priests, was tolerated. " The smallest portion of the work falls to us; " each day I glean but a scanty crop for eternity. " The greater part of the sick do not go to con- " fession, and the priest is there but a deputy of " the Church, timidly looking around to see if " perchance there be a soul belonging to the flock. " . . . . Here and there one or two go to " confession. Others are in a dying state, sight-

" less and dumb. I lay my hand upon their brow,
" and confiding in the divine mercy, I utter the
" words of absolution.

" I seldom leave without feeling glad at having
" come. Yesterday, a woman had just been car-
" ried in ; her husband, a soldier, was standing at
" the head of her bed. I approached, and as I
" am dressed as a layman, the soldier asked me in
" a whisper whether it would be possible to get a
" priest. *I am one.* It does one's heart good to
" come just in time to save a soul, and be of
" use to a man." *

Towards the end of this same year, and subsequently to his rupture with M. de la Mennais,
he fell into a dream that had often haunted him
during the most busy part of his previous life.
He wanted to become a country priest in a distant
province ; and he mentioned, why I do not know,
Franche-Comté.

" I wish," he said, " to bury myself in the

---

* 22nd April, 1832.

" depths of the country, to live only for a small
" flock, and to seek my joy in God and in the
" fields.   People will see clearly whether I am a
" simple and unambitious man.   Farewell, great
" labours ! farewell, renown and great men !   I
" have learnt the vanity of all this, and my only
" desire is to lead a good and obscure life.   Some
" day when Montalembert shall have grown grey
" in the midst of ingratitude and celebrity, he will
" come and contemplate on my brow—the remains
" of a youth passed together.   We will shed tears
" together by the presbytery hearth ; he will do me
" justice before we both die.   I will bless his
" children. . . . .*   As for me, a poor
" Catholic priest, I shall have neither children to
" take my place, growing up under my eyes, nor
" home, nor church resplendent with learning and
" sanctity.   Born in ordinary times, I shall go my
" way through the world among the things which
" do not live in the memory of man.   I shall en-

---

* 9th April, 1832.

" deavour to be good, simple, pious, looking
" forward to the future with disinterested confi-
" dence, since I shall not see it; labouring for
" those who will perhaps see it; and not mur-
" muring against Providence, who might without
" injustice heap more evils upon a life so devoid
" of merit."*

But M. de Quelen, Archbishop of Paris, kept
him in his diocese. This prelate long testified
towards the young priest ordained by him a really
fatherly kindness, in spite of the vast difference of
their natures, their origin, and their political views.
The good pastor assigned this son, who had come
sad and wounded out of the unequal contest, a
sweet and peaceful retreat, by again offering him
the chaplaincy of the Visitation, already held by
him in 1827. Lacordaire lived during three years
in the modest apartment given him at the convent. His mother came there to live with him,
and died in his arms. God had however given

---

* 11th December, 1832.

him another who was destined to go down into the grave but a few years before himself.

On his return from La Chesnaie, I had had the happiness to introduce him to Madame Swetchine,* who soon saw in him her chosen son, and who showered upon this young but storm-tried head all the ingenious care and deep sympathy of her lofty and upright soul. He has himself related the impression she made upon him. " Her soul " was to mine what the shore is to the plank " shattered by the waves ; and I still remember, " after the lapse of twenty-five years, all the light " and strength she afforded to a young man un- " known to her. Her counsel preserved me alike " from despondency and the opposite extreme."

She became and remained, during a quarter

---

* A Russian lady of rank, who, having become a Catholic, came to Paris in 1814, and remained there till her death in 1857. Her house was the resort of the most brilliant society in Paris, as well as of all the personages of note in the religious world. Count de Falloux has published a memoir of her in two volumes, besides two other volumes of her *Correspondance.*—[*Translator's Note.*]

of a century, the guide, the counsellor, the physician of this agitated and tried mind, which at once became calm, and gradually and progressively yielded to so sweet an influence.

Nothing ever disturbed the blessed union of these two souls, of this mother and son, so worthy of each other, and both so well described by Lacordaire's saying upon Madame Swetchine, " I " never met anyone in whom such breadth and " boldness of thought was allied to such firm " faith."

There it was then, in a narrow winding street of the Quartier Latin, at the foot of the hill of Sainte Généviève, that Lacordaire lived more than three years. There it is that my memory sees him : greater, more admirable, perhaps, than before the House of Peers, at the French Academy, or even at Notre-Dame. I see him growing daily in calmness and recollection; in prayer, study, charity, solitude; in a grave, simple, unnoticed life, truly hidden in God. That is the spot where he matured his genius, and whence darted that eagle whose flight has so far outdone that of all his rivals.

During the very thickest of the fight, he had ever praised a peaceful and uniform life. " Happy " the man," he wrote, " who is born and dies " under the same roof without ever leaving it. " But such are no longer to be found in the world; " the rich themselves are wanderers like the rest. " Palaces as well as cabins have ceased to be " heirlooms ; we are like those woodcutters who " make out a shelter for themselves for a few " days at the foot of a tree, and who, having " consumed everything around it, cut down the " trunk against which they rested their heads, " and move away. Let us, at least, form to " ourselves an eternal friendship in the midst of " this world, where nothing is lasting and un- " changeable ; let our hearts serve us as ancestral " homes."

Behold him, then, under a roof which was neither that of his fathers, nor that which was to shelter him for ever, but a modest and quiet one. He enjoyed it without thinking of the future. " In the long run, habits alone captivate the soul. " Novelty ceases to be novelty ; what is old ends

H

" by acquiring novelty, so multiplied are the
" memories and ideas with which it peoples the
" soul."*

He clung to it, and resisted every appeal. He
twice refused the editorship of the paper called
L' Univers, which was then being founded. He
declined, too, a chair in the Catholic University
of Louvain, whose founders have for ever
honored that creation of the faith and liberty
of the nineteenth century, by calling thither the
most illustrious champion of the alliance between
religion and liberty. Unknown to the vulgar,
misunderstood by many, he was as yet unconscious
of himself; he clung to solitude with a passion
the expression of which is the ever recurring
theme of his letters. " I have always stood
" in need of solitude, even in order to tell
" the strength of my love.† . . . .
" My days are all alike. I work regularly morn-
' ing and afternoon. I see no one, except a few

---

* 3rd December, 1834.   † September 1831.

" provincial ecclesiastics, who drop in now and
" again to see me. It is with joy that I see
' solitude begin to reign around me,—it is my
" element, my life.* Nothing is achieved without
" solitude,—such is my great axiom. The heart
" suffers, even when it is not lost, by continual
" contact with strangers ; it is like a flower car-
" ried out of doors.† Man forms himself in his
" own interior, and nowhere else!" Still, a certain intuition of the future to which he was
destined was combined with this passionate love
of solitude, and appeared to his friends to break
upon his soul, from time to time, like a streak
of lightning in the night. " To preach and write,
" to live in studious solitude, such is the desire
" of my soul. The future will complete my justi-
" fication, and still more so the judgment of
" God.‡ Every man has his day, if he only
" knows how to wait, and not thwart the de-
" signs of Providence."§

---

* 8th September, 1833.　† 15th February, 1834.
‡ 1st October, 1834.　§ 30th June, 1833.

This day was about to dawn for him, and he was soon to enter upon a sphere of public activity which seemed to have most attraction for him, and to be best adapted to his talents.

He said so with a sincerity which nothing during his whole life ever gainsaid. " I am not " and cannot be ambitious ; for all the high po- " sitions in the Church are either pastoral or ad- " ministrative posts, absolutely incompatible with " my tastes. I never shall have, and never want " to have, any functions. But one must turn one- " self to account, because conscience obliges us."*

Feeling himself born an orator, he, like every ordinary priest, tried the pulpit. He preached for the first time at S. Roch, in that same church which was destined to hear, nineteen years later, the last scathing accents of his voice at Paris.

It was in the spring of 1833. I was present together with MM. de Corcelles, Ampère, and others, who must remember it as well as myself.

---

* 19th August, 1833.

He failed completely, and we all said on leaving, "*He is a talented man, but will never* "*make a preacher.*" He himself thought so. "It " is clear to me that I have neither enough bodi- " ly strength, suppleness of mind, nor sufficient " knowledge of the world, where I have always " lived, and shall continue to live solitary; in " fine, that *I have enough of nothing* that goes to " make up a preacher in the full force of the " word. But I may one day be called to a mis- " sion which the youth of our country require, " and which may be specially consecrated to " them. . . . . If my voice is to serve the " Church, it will be simply in the region of apo- " logy, in which the beauties and greatness of re- " ligion are set forth, as well as its historical and " controversial side, in order to give minds some " inkling of the greatness of Christianity, and pre- " pare them for the faith."*

This mission, *exclusively consecrated* to youth,

------

* 19th August, 1888.

soon presented itself: he was asked to give conferences to the scholars of the most unpretending
of the Paris colleges, the Collège Stanislas.   They
were begun on the 19th of January, 1834: at the
second, the chapel was unable to hold the crowd
that pressed in, and a gallery had to be erected.
" It is a growing plant," he observed, at the end
of the first month.   There exists but a very short
analysis of these first essays.   But in these un-
finished notes, the great features of the orator of
Notre-Dame are distinguishable : striking originality, insinuating and real passion, the impetuous
rush of thought and expression, tenderness and
irony.   I have heard from others that one day he
said, for the benefit of certain scoffers, " Gentle-
" men, God has made you witty, very witty
" indeed, to show you how little He cares for
" the wit of man."

However, it is certain that his name and fame
were growing rapidly : but still he met with
marked and continually increasing opposition.
" Here," he wrote, towards the close of this first
series of conferences, " I am looked upon as a
" hair-brained republican, an incorrigible offender,

" and a thousand other delicate things of the
" same sort. . . . .   There are some ecclesiastics
" who charge me, not precisely with atheism,
" but with not having pronounced the name of
" Jesus Christ one single time. . . . . . .   I scorn
" the annoyance given to me : I fulfil my duty
" as a man and a priest : I live alone, in continual
" study, calm, trustful in God and the future.
" Nothing can be done without the help of the
" Church and of time.   Had the Abbé de la Men-
" nais but willed, what a glorious opening for
" him ! He was at the height of his glory, and
" I have never been able to understand how a
" man of that cast could have ignored the
" value of what God left for him.   The religious
" task forsaken by him is so grand, so easy, so
" much above all others, that in three months,
" in Paris, I have moved more hearts and heads
" than I could possibly have done during the
" fifteen years of the Restoration."*

---

* 17th April, 1834.

Denounced as he was at Rome, denounced to Government, and especially to the Archbishop of Paris, he was obliged in the first place to suspend his conferences, and then to give up the idea of taking them up again during the winter of 1834. M. de Quelen, who at first authorized this second attempt, finally stopped it. Lacordaire did not murmur, even to his most intimate friends: "Obedience is painful," he wrote to me, "but experience has taught me that "sooner or later it is rewarded, and that God "alone knows what is good for us.* . . . . "The light breaks in upon him who submits, as "upon one who opens his eyes."

He had not left the Visitandines. He was still leading his quiet life there, when, by an un-accountable determination, M. de Quelen, who had been mistaken in applying to the apparent submission of M. de la Mennais the text, "*Vir* "*obediens loquetur victorias*," gave Lacordaire a

------

* 12th November, 1834.

signal opportunity of proving its truth. Upon the repeated instances of a deputation of law students, at whose head was Ozanam,* the Archbishop called upon the preacher of the Collège Stanislas to mount the pulpit of Notre-Dame,† and to give the conferences which had been organized for the youth of the schools the preceding year without any great result.

Lacordaire ascended, then, for the first time that pulpit since immortalized by him, and delivered during the years 1835 and 1836 the fifteen famous conferences *on the Church* which are in everybody's hands.

We may say that if never unequal to, he

---

* This young man, born in 1812, who became later Professor of Foreign Literature in the University of Paris, is one of the most distinguished and most justly popular of French Catholic writers. He died in 1853. His works have been published in eight volumes. Amongst them are particularly to be noticed *Histoire de la Civilisation Chrétienne au Cinquième Siècle, Etudes Germaniques, Les Poëtes Franciscains en Italie, Dante et la Philosophie Catholic au XIII. Siècle.*—[*Translator's Note.*]

† The Metropolitan Church of the Arch-Diocese of Paris.

rarely, except in the conferences at Toulouse in 1854, surpassed the splendour and solidity of this first series of discourses. M. de Quelen, who assisted at all these sermons, and who, for the first time since the outrages which had been heaped upon him after the revolution of July,* found himself in presence of the world, was delighted with a triumph which so nobly avenged him, by coupling him with the popularity of this rising star.

One day, rising from his archiepiscopal throne in presence of that immense audience, he greeted his young client with the title of *New Prophet*.

We all know what were the audiences at Notre-Dame : never had those venerable walls seen the like. Let us remind our readers that the core of them was first formed by the Society of St. Vincent of Paul, which had just been given

---

* M. de Quelen, Archbishop of Paris from 1823 till 1839, had been very unpopular during the last years of the Restoration, and when the revolution of July broke out, his palace was sacked and destroyed, and he himself obliged to take refuge in a convent, where he remained for several years.

to the Church by Ozanam, one of those whom
Lacordaire most loved, and of whom he said but
quite recently, "*He is an ancestor!*" The ranks
of this glorious band swelled and multiplied ten-
fold around the pulpit of Notre-Dame. It there
drank in that spirit which carried it, until yesterday intact, respected and blessed through our
revolutions and our struggles. Lacordaire was
next to Ozanam, and with him its father. He
might have said of it, *Apollo plantavit, ego rigavi,
sed Deus incrementum dedit.*

Speaking one day at Notre-Dame of this
youthful legion "which has put its chastity under
" the shield of charity, the loveliest of virtues
" under the loveliest of guardians," he said:
" What blessings will not this youthful chivalry
" draw down upon France; this chivalry of
" purity, and of brotherhood in the cause of the
" poor! . . . . Let the gratitude of the
" country be at least the safeguard of their
" liberty." This prayer has not been heard.
How pitiable is our time and our country! The
dear and glorious apostle of Catholic youth was
wasting away, a prey to the most intense agonies,

upon the couch from which he was to rise no more, and already underhand calumny had beaten down his work; already the death-blow had been dealt out to the purest and most spontaneous offspring of Christian democracy by one of those giddy, cruel hands into which God puts human power when He wants to show man how little He makes of it.*

Let us imagine Lacordaire alive, with a free press, in presence of such an act, and we shall be able to figure to ourselves the punishment he would have dealt out with that pen which had branded minor criminals with those scorching invectives, whose echo was still ringing in the pulpit of Notre-Dame: *He, this sub-prefect !*†

---

* This passage alludes to the dissolution of the Society of St. Vincent de Paul, by the order of Napoleon III., and by the advice of M. de Persigny, Minister of the Interior in 1861. The Society, founded under King Louis Philippe in 1833, by Ozanam and eleven other young students (amongst whom was Count de Montalembert), had refused to accept an official director or chief, named by the Emperor, like the Grand Master he at the same time granted to the Freemasons, in the person of Marshal Magnan.

† See page 22.

CHAPTER V.

SECOND STAY AT ROME.—HE ENTERS THE ORDER OF
FRIARS PREACHERS, AND RESTORES THE ORDER IN
FRANCE.—CONFERENCES AT NOTRE-DAME.—LIBERTY
OF EDUCATION AND ASSOCIATION.

PUBLICITY, popularity, and glory were thus
becoming his portion.

Nothing was wanting that could content and
intoxicate him; and this at the age of thirty-
three years! But by one of those wonderful
pieces of intuition, for which he was particularly
remarkable, he saw that silence and solitude
were still necessary for him. He drew up at
the very climax of his triumph. "I leave in
" the hands of my bishop this School of Notre-
" Dame, founded by him and by you, by the

" pastor and the people. This double suffrage
" has for a moment lighted on my brow : suffer
" me to withdraw from it, and to live for a time
" alone in presence of God and my weakness."
These words ended his second lenten station in
April, 1836. His mind once made up, he declined, notwithstanding the instances of his archbishop, to mount the pulpit again, and left for
Rome.

He returned to Rome, rewarded beyond all
hope for the sacrifice he had made four years
previously in leaving it and M. de la Mennais
behind. But he returned, ever humble, simple,
and retiring. "It is a banishment," he wrote to
me, "for I was never blind to the fact, that two
" years spent out of France in solitude and study
" would be a hard matter ; but it was necessary.
" We must even thank God for having attached
" pain to everything, in order that there may
" be room for merit in everything."* We again

---

* August 15th, 1836. This same letter contains a passage which will be read with interest. " Having an oppor-

met there, and lived together, peaceful, united, and happy, on the site of our old divisions and sufferings.

I left him there in the spring of 1837. He, too, was intending to return to France; but the cholera broke out with fearful violence at the very moment of his intended departure.

In presence of this scourge and the general desertion, he put himself at the disposal of the cardinal-vicar. The letter in which he communicated this resolution to me ended thus: "If "I die you will cherish my memory. But care "not to take up its defence: it will not be worth "fighting for."*

To what will he turn during this new period

" tunity to examine the Jesuits closely, I have learnt to " know them better, and I have sincerely admired their faith, " their good breeding, the ease with which they take in every- " thing, and rise to the level of every position, which was " always one of their characteristics; finally, a real freedom " from political passions, and a readiness to recognize order " wherever it is, and to uphold religion above every other " interest."

* 11th August, 1837.

of solitude and silence ?   Madame Swetchine said
of him : "I know no virtue more admirable than
" his, nor any more likely to rise to sanctity, if
" only it can bend and endure obscurity." *

It is precisely this doubt that he will answer,
by curbing his manly nature, and embracing a
monastic rule at the height of his popularity.

Five years from the date of his first conferences, we see him re-appear in the pulpit of
Notre-Dame, clothed in the Dominican habit.

The motives which led to his monastic vocation, the singular and critical circumstances
accompanying it, the reasons which induced him
to choose the order of Friars Preachers rather
than any other, have just been related by him
in a document which will seal his renown, and
reckon, I venture to affirm, among the noblest
monuments of Catholic history.   The bequest of
a real miracle of moral courage, dictated by him
with unparalleled sureness and rapidity during

---

* *Lettres Familières,* p. 201.

the last month of his mortal life, these pages, each of which was either preceded or followed by excruciating suffering, and to which his agony alone put a stop, will show us his style in its perfection, and his masculine genius lighted up, as it were, "*by that terrible flame which is kindled* "*for the dying.*" * I extract from this important document, the publication of which has been entrusted to the Abbé Perreyve, a few lines, which say all :

" My long stay at Rome allowing me much " time for reflection, I studied myself and the " general wants of the Church. . . . . " It seemed to me as though, since the destruc- " tion of the religious orders, she had lost half " her strength. I saw at Rome the magnificent " remains of those institutions founded by the " greatest saints ; I saw seated upon the pontifical " throne, after so many others of the same robe, " a monk called from the cloister of St. Gregory " the Great.

---

* *Saint Simon.*

" History, more eloquent even than the spec-
" tacle of Rome, showed me, from the catacombs
" downwards, that incomparable succession of
" cells, monasteries, abbeys, schools of learning
" and prayer, sown broadcast from the sands of
" Thebais to the extremities of Ireland, from
" the fragrant isles of Provence to the cold plains
" of Poland and Russia. She named to me
" St. Antony, St. Basil, St. Augustine, St. Martin,
" St. Benedict, St. Columbanus, St. Bernard,
" St. Francis of Assizium, St. Dominic, St. Ig-
" natius, as the patriarchs of those numerous
" families which had filled deserts, forests, camps,
" even to the chair of St. Peter, with their heroic
" virtues.

" Beneath this brilliant zone, which is as it
" were the ' milky way ' of the Church, I descried
" the creative principle in the three vows of
" poverty, chastity, and obedience, the key-stones
" of the Gospel and of the perfect imitation of
" Jesus Christ.

" It was in vain that corruption had, now
" here, now there, eaten into these venerable
" institutions. This corruption itself was but

" the decay of ancient virtue; just as the mon-
" archs of forests, untouched by the axe, may
" be seen falling under the weight of a life
" drawn from too great a distance to withstand
" caducity. Must we believe that the time was
" come when those great monuments of faith,
" and those divine tokens of the love of God and
" mankind were to disappear? Were we to be-
" lieve that the whirlwind of revolution, instead
" of being a temporary visitation upon their
" faults, had been the sword and seal of death?
" I could not believe it: every creation of God
" is of its nature immortal, and a virtue is no
" more lost in the world than a star in the
" heavens.

" Whilst wandering, then, through Rome, and
" praying in her basilicas, I became convinced
" that the greatest service to be done to Christen-
" dom was an effort for the resurrection of the
" religious orders. But this conviction, although
" as clear as the Gospel to me, left me hesitating
" and trembling when I came to consider my in-
" equality to so great a work. My faith, God be
" thanked, was deep-rooted: I loved Jesus Christ

" and his Church beyond all created things.
" Before loving God I had loved glory, and
" nothing else. Still when I looked into myself,
" I discovered nothing corresponding to my idea
" of a founder or restorer of an order. When
" I looked upon those giants of Christian piety
" and strength, my soul sank within me. The
" simple thought of sacrificing my liberty to a
" rule and to superiors terrified me. The child
" of an age which scarcely knows what obedience
" s, independence had been my couch and my
" guide. How was I to change myself suddenly
" into one docile of heart, and look for light in
" submission alone?

" Nor was this all : external obstacles stood
" like mountains in my way. . . . . No asso-
" ciation, even literary or artistic, being tolerated
" in France without previous permission, this
" extremity of slavery, which had been sub-
" mitted to, afforded prejudice an easy means of
" resisting every appeal to natural or public law.
" What was to be done in a country in which
" religious liberty, admitted by all as a principle
" sacred to the new world, was however power-

" less to shield in the heart of the citizen the
" invisible act of a promise made to God, and
" where such a promise, discovered by tyrannical
" interrogatories, was sufficient to deprive him
" of the benefit of common justice ?*   When a
" people is reduced to this pass, and every liberty
" is looked upon as a privilege of the unbeliever
" against the believer, is there any hope of ever
" seeing reign among them equity, peace, and sta-
" bility, or any civilization other than that of
" material progress ?

   " Thus, as may be seen, wherever I looked
" nothing but dangers met my gaze, and less
" fortunate than Christopher Columbus, I could
" not descry a single plank to carry me to the
" shores of liberty.   My only resource was the
" boldness which animated the first Christians,
" and unshaken confidence in the Almighty arm

---

* This alludes to the *test* or *pledge*, which, previous to the
law granting freedom of education in 1850, was exacted from
all clergymen employed in public education, in order to prevent their belonging to any religious order or association not
authorized by the State.

" of God. . . . . There is ever in the
" heart of man, in the state of minds, in the
" tide of opinion, in all laws, all things, and all
" times, a point open to the action of God.

" The great art is to discover it, and turn it
" to account, whilst relying on the secret and
" invisible power of God as the' spring of one's
" courage and hopes. Christianity has never
" bearded the world; has never insulted nature
" and reason; has never converted its light into
" a power which blinds by irritating; but equally
" mild and bold, calm and energetic, tender and
" intrepid, it has ever found the way to the genius
" of generations; and until the end of time its
" conquests will ever be brought about by the
" same means.

" Encouraged by these thoughts, it seemed
" to me as though the whole of my previous life,
" and even my very faults had in a certain
" measure prepared for me an entrance into the
" heart of my country and my day.

" I asked myself whether I should not be
" guilty in losing this opportunity by a timidity
" which would be of no use but to myself, and

" whether the greatness of the sacrifice was not
" a reason for attempting it. . . . .

" Urged on by the state of things, and by
" a grace stronger than myself, I made up my
" mind, but the sacrifice was a terrible one.
" Whilst I had quitted the world without a pang
" to enter into the priesthood, it cost me a vast
" deal to add to the priesthood the burden of
" the religious life. Still in the second case, as
" in the first, my consent once given, I knew
" neither weakness nor regret, and I went boldly
" forward to meet the trials which awaited me."

It will not be uninteresting to place side by
side with this grand picture, traced by the dying
hand of this religious at the end of his monastic
career, the simple lines in which, twenty-three
years before, he announced his determination. " I
" am going to return to Rome, chiefly with a view
" to enter into the Dominican order, and with
" the intention of restoring it in France, if such
" should be the will of God. I think this act
" is the reason of my existence, the result of
" all that God has hitherto done for me, the
" secret of his graces, of my trials and my ex-

" perience. I am like a man who has gained
" credit, and who can turn it to noble account.
" Without my past I should be powerless; and
" a continuation of the past would be out of
" proportion to the graces God has given me.
" Pray for me that He may give me the grace
" of which I stand in need, and that He may
" clear away difficulties."*

Four years later he wrote from the cell of an
Italian monastery these lines, which no religious
will read without emotion :

"I am in possession of an impregnable fort-
" ress ; henceforth no one can give me or take me,
" or imagine that he gives me or takes me. . . . .
" . . . . One must have struggled as I
" have against an individual and difficult position,
" in order fully to appreciate the benefits of
" real religious life. The misfortunes through
" which I have passed, and through which so
" many others are toiling, make my present life

1st June, 1838.

" so happy, that were I destined to spend here
" the rest of my life with the brothers God has
" given me, I should consider myself more than
" repaid for my poor labours in the service of
" the Church.   I am profiting largely by the
" spiritual life and theological study : our Thomist
" school is so admirable.   Would that I had long
" ago drunk of these deep waters ! . . . . I believe
" that some of my enemies are partly of my own
" making ; but the general situation necessarily
" implies fearful opposition.

" It is therefore possible that I may die when
" I have opened the breach for my Dominicans,
" and when I shall be no longer anything but an
" obstacle.   God raises up special men for special
" purposes : He does not mind their small intrinsic
" worth, provided they are suited to his ends, and
" He casts them aside when they get to be in the
" way." *

In the only sermon preached by him in 1841,

---

* Bosco.   14th September, 1838.

at Notre-Dame, he took for his subject, *The Vocation of the French Nation*, and only casually alluded to his own religious vocation. But he intended, by mounting the pulpit of the Metropolitan Church at Paris, in his Dominican garb, to introduce into France that religious habit, which she had not seen for half a century.*

He appeared then with shaven head and white habit in the midst of six thousand young men : he was as eloquent as of old, and no serious opposition was manifested. Government did, it is true, show some signs of uneasiness, and a slight inclination to forbid his appearance. Lacordaire showed neither fear nor self-sufficiency.

He entered into a kind of negotiation with the Keeper of the Seals, the then Minister of

----

* He wore it for the first time in the pulpit of the Church of Bordeaux, where he preached during six consecutive months, thanks to the energetic protection of the Archbishop, Monseigneur Donnet, who, the first among the bishops of France, had the honour of offering to the habit of the friar-preacher frank and public hospitality.

Public Worship, M. Martin (du *Nord*), and disarmed him by his simplicity, his candour, and
the firmness of his attitude.

I was their intermediary, and I find in one of
the letters which he gave me to communicate to
the minister this passage : " The stability of the
" government, the maintenance of those liberties
" which experience has shown to be necessary to
" France, the propagation of the gospel, of which
" the Church is the sole and infallible depositary,
" such are, in the temporal and spiritual order,
" my thoughts and desires.

" A stranger to all party-spirit, I have ever
" striven to honour my faith by confining it to the
" region of justice and good-will.

" Public opinion has rewarded me by raising
" me far above the place attainable by my feeble
" capacity, and if government has not hitherto
" known me such as I am, I perhaps owe it to
" another merit, that of never having sought its
" favours. To-day that I can no longer aspire to
" anything, I am free to make this observation,
" and I avail myself of this liberty to reassure

" your Excellency, touching my opinions and my
" plans." *

During the three years which followed this
reinstatement of monastic liberty in the pulpit
of Notre-Dame, Lacordaire's life was spent partly
in France, partly in Italy. In Italy, by reason
of serious trials, which it is not my intention to
judge, nor even to relate, he was obliged to
transfer his French noviciate from Rome to
Bosco in Piedmont, where he lived happy and
peaceful under the protection of Charles Albert's
government, and whence he went one day to
preach to the brigade of Savoy, in the fortress
of Alessandria.

In France, whither he returned every winter,
he preached with ever increasing success, at
Bordeaux and Nancy, and in the latter town he
founded, under the shield of common liberty, and
of the inviolability of private property, the first
of the seven houses of his restored order.†

---

* 2nd August, 1842.   † January 1843.

In the meantime, the question of liberty of education, (so stoutly put forth by him twelve years previously in the *Avenir*, and before the House of Peers,) after having lain by for some time, had been again taken up with fresh vigour, and had powerfully aroused public attention.

In the wake of this question, naturally followed that of freedom of association, since communities alone could really meet the requirements of free instruction.

Whilst the episcopacy and the Catholic publicists demanded the liberty promised by the Charta, with all its consequences, the orators and writers of the university party (infinitely more numerous) violently defended their monopoly, and turned, against the Jesuits particularly, the unpopularity which the heirs of the perverse doctrines and cruel persecutions of the eighteenth century are ever ready to stir up against religious orders.

" *We owe them nothing but expulsion,*" exclaimed a deputy but too famous for his interruptions ; and this cry seemed to the crowd of so-called liberals the best answer to the demands made, in the name of liberty and equality, in favour of religious associations.

The Government, timid rather than ill-willed, and at bottom resolved to persecute no one, allowed itself to be carried away and mastered by the tide of anti-religious passions.

The white habit of the Dominican, worn in the pulpit and in the street, was no longer looked upon by ministers with the uneasy but kindly neutrality of 1841 ; it created serious anxiety, which showed itself in protests and threats, as a prelude to more serious measures.

At this conjuncture, Monseigneur Affre, Archbishop of Paris, invited Father Lacordaire to resume his conferences, and in spite of the instances of Government, the prelate who was, later on, to sacrifice his life with such calm and modest heroism,* upheld with invincible firmness the liberty of

---

* Mgr. Affre was killed during the frightful struggle of June, 1848. He had gone, attended by a single vicar-general, and bearing a green branch in his hand, to exhort the insurgents to listen to the pacific proposals of the National Assembly. A ball fired from behind one of the barricades

the evangelical word. In December 1843, Lacordaire again ascended the pulpit of Notre-Dame, which he was to fill for eight consecutive years, until the *coup d'état* of 1851.

These were the heroic times of our religious and liberal struggles. We saw a Dominican and a Jesuit, both illustrious, both above the very shadow of jealous rivalry, teach youth the art of trampling upon human respect, and lead it on to the practice of the faith, as well as to the conquest of the civil rights of Catholicism. Each winter Lacordaire gave seven or eight conferences, during the months of December and January ; he then went to preach the Lenten station in some provincial town, Grenoble, Lyons, or Strasburg ; leaving Father Ravignan to take his place at Notre-Dame, and prepare, by his Lenten station and retreat in Holy Week, the way for those Easter communions which have been ever since the glory and conso-

---

mortally wounded him. He fell and exclaimed, "*May my* "*blood be the last shed!*" And so it was, for the battle ceased on the next day.—[*Translator's Note.*]

lation of the Church of Paris, and which forced some people to say, as early as 1844, " We must "lay the hand of Voltaire upon these men." They did their best to put their saying into execution, but with liberty, one can make light even of Voltaire.

This, the first station of Lacordaire at Notre-Dame, since the struggle had grown hot, ended only in February 1844. He himself called it " the most perilous and decisive of his campaigns." It succeeded beyond all expectation. It fortified and inflamed the courage of all. It was a worthy prelude to the parliamentary struggle of that memorable year and the following one, in which the religious orders, violently assailed in the tribune, were defended there as they had not been defended since 1789.*

The resistance offered by Catholics to the

---

* Those desirous of forming some idea of this defence can do nothing better than look into the Count de Montalembert's own magnificent speeches, to be found in his works, published by Lecoffre, of Paris.—[*Translator's Note.*]

passions and prejudices of an illogical liberalism visibly increased, thanks to the union and courage of the episcopacy, thanks also to the resolute attitude of Catholics in the elections. Their action was both dignified and enlightened ; their influence upon modern society became daily more uniform and more powerful.

This state of things lasted until the revolution of February, which at first hurried on this salutary movement, then diverted, and finally annihilated it. Not a voice was then heard in our ranks to hinder or carp at it. " We both served Christian " freedom under the standard of public freedom," said Lacordaire, with happy terseness in his notice upon Father de Ravignan. The latter, in an eloquent, calm, and dignified publication, demanded as a citizen, and in the name of the Charta, in the name of that liberty of conscience guaranteed to all, the right to be and to call himself a Jesuit. Lastly, the illustrious priest who has since won the first place among the episcopacy of our day, spoke as follows, with the universal assent of the clergy and faithful :

K

" What is meant by the spirit of the French
" Revolution ? . . . .

" Are we to understand free institutions, liberty
" of conscience, political liberty, civil and indi-
" vidual liberty, the liberty of families, freedom of
" education, liberty of opinion, equality before the
" law, the equal distribution of public taxes and
" burthens ?

" *All this, we not only honestly accept, but all*
" *this we call for in the broad daylight of public*
" *discussion.*

" These liberties, so dear to those who charge
" us with not loving them, we champion ; we
" ask them FOR OURSELVES AS WELL AS FOR
" OTHERS.

" At the present moment what are we doing,
" other than rendering homage to the true spirit
" of the French Revolution, by claiming its advan-
" tages, and demanding the freedom of instruction
" promised by the Charta, in the name of every
" lawful religious liberty ?

" We accept, we invoke the principles and
" liberties put forth in 1789. . . . .

" I think this, and I say so, without hesitation,

" to the men of 1789, as well as to the men of
" to-day, who would fain fasten upon us the yoke
" of an absurd oppression, and who invoke against
" us alone the impotent laws of a decayed juris-
" prudence.

" I will say without any hesitation, even
" should this saying be considered bold in the
" mouth of a priest, who, I will add, is no re-
" volutionist:

" *You brought about the Revolution of* 1789,
" *without us and against us, but* FOR US, *God so*
" *willing it, in spite of you.*"*

Preachers, orators, writers, all unanimous,
added their voice to that of the episcopacy in
this cry for religious liberty; not, as Lacordaire
himself so well explained it, religious liberty
after the fashion of Luther, but " liberty after
" the modern mind, which has never lessened, by
" a single inch, the spiritual jurisdiction of the
" Roman pontiff: which is nothing else but re-

---

* Dupanloup. *De la Pacification religieuse*, pp. 286, 287,
300, 304; re-edited 1861.

" spect for others' convictions, which has no
" bearing upon dogmatic or moral questions, upon
" worship, upon the authority of Christianity ;
" but which simply deprives Christianity of the
" aid of the civil power in seeking out and
" punishing heresy, confiding in the inborn and
" divine power of faith, which cannot fail for
" want of the sword in its combat with error."*

Catholics had thus arrayed on their side the
past, the present, and the future, by the aid of
one single weapon—publicity, which is the voice
and right hand of history, as Lacordaire once
said in one of those oratorical movements which
electrified his audience : " Publicity is a power
" which forces the enemies of a cause to speak
" out, and to help, in spite of themselves, in
" the authentic formation of a history which
" they detest, and would fain annihilate.   In
" vain ; publicity forces them ; they must speak,
" and even whilst calumniating must say enough

---

* *Discourse upon the Law of History.*

" of the truth to render its destruction impos-
" sible.

" This it is, gentlemen, which saves history;
" there is nothing in the world more cordially
" hated: the oppressors of the people and the
" enemies of God strive for nothing more than
" for the destruction of history; they attempt to
" gag it, they shut up their victim within the nar-
" row and lonesome walls of the dungeon; they
" surround it with cannon and lances, with all the
" apparatus of intimidation and fear; but pub-
" licity is stronger than all empires, it bears
" away with it those even who abominate it; it
" forces them to speak, their cannon are turned
" aside, their lances are lowered, and history
" marches past!"*

Lacordaire thus saw men and circumstances
conspire towards the realization and vindication
of his youthful dreams. He enjoyed this unexpected triumph without being either overweening

---

* *Conferences of Notre-Dame. Sur la Puissance publique de Jésus Christ.*

or elated. . . . . " The accomplishment
" of duty with courage and simplicity is still
" the surest way to win from mankind the justice
" of true admiration. . . . ."

"Time is necessary for everything," he wrote,
" let us only be always ready without fore-
" stalling the hour marked out by Providence.
" What a difference between 1834 and 1844!
" Ten years have sufficed to change the scene
" completely.* . . . . The way we have
" made in this last campaign in unity, strength,
" and prospects, is scarcely credible ; even sup-
" posing the cause of freedom of education to
" be lost for fifty years, we have gained even
" more than itself, for we have won the arm
" which gives it, and with it those liberties ne-
" cessary for the salvation of France and of the
" world. †

"If the poor Abbé de la Mennais had but
" known how to wait, what a moment for him!

---

* 15th May, 1844.   † 28th June, 1844.

" Alas! we so often told him so! he would be
" greater than ever . . . . All that was
" required was humility and confidence in the
" Church.   Up to the very last moment the
" cause was a splendid one, indeed so much so
" that it is now won. . . . .

" Younger and more simple, we have accepted
" the direction of the Church ; we have candidly
" acknowledged the exaggeration of our style and
" even of our ideas ; and God, who probes the reins
" and the heart, has cast upon us a look of mercy ;
" He has been good enough not to cast us away,
" and even to make use of us.

" There never was since the foundation of
" the Church an example of a greater reward
" granted to submission, beside a more terrible
" chastisement inflicted upon rebellion."*

His advice, too, bore the stamp of prudence
and of that practical turn which always distinguished him.   He exhorted us not to be eager

* 11th March, 23rd June, 1844.

to get everything at once; to hold patiently the ground already gained, and not to plunge into theories without beginning or end; above all not to give our enemies a pretext for proclaiming that we wanted to upset French society.

He himself entered into the controversy neither by word nor deed, and in none of his conferences is the slightest allusion to it to be found. It was in this warful year of 1844 that he pronounced his famous discourses upon chastity, which silenced his most stubborn detractors, and remain, despite time and criticism, like an exquisite pearl that no breath can tarnish.

But the universal popularity of his eloquence, the immense audiences which flocked around the pulpit whenever he mounted it, were arguments far more eloquent than any discourse upon politics or public law. It sufficed for him to prove his victory by his preaching at Paris and in the rest of France, and by his conquest of the right of living in community, and wearing the habit of his order; which right no one ever dared to dispute in the different places where he and his friars dwelt.

He was, moreover, determined to hold till the end to the course which displayed in him that civic courage so rare in France, and yet so necessary, especially for Catholics.

He stated formally, in founding his different houses, his intention of fighting over again, if need be, the battle of the free school: "Let "them put you out of your house by force; "return as soon as possible, protest publicly, "appeal to the law for the disposal of your "property; the right of disposal recovered, re- "turn with those belonging to you."

Such was the line of conduct he had marked out for himself, and which he recommended to all menaced communities. Fortunately the moderation and morality of the king and his ministers, on the one hand, and on the other the all-powerful influence of free discussion, rendered this judicial struggle unnecessary.

Seventeen years later, when reviewing on his death-bed his recollections of this great moment of his life, he said :

"The religious habit has acquired for the "future the right of citizenship in all the pulpits

" and on every point of France, which it had
" lost in 1790. This was in truth the first con-
" quest of the Church of France in the thorny
" path of liberty.

" It was neither gained nor ratified by a law,
" but was the result of the cry of conscience,
" the hidden strength of the Gospel, and the
" moderation of government. That government
" was desirous of not being intolerant, and as
" soon as it saw public peace safe, it tacitly
" consented to what it could have hindered only
" by violence, which it was unwilling to employ.

" As soon as among a people there is a real
" leaven of liberty, that leaven bears down, even
" unknown to itself, all opposition ; and as truth
" begets truth, and justice justice, so in the ne-
" cessary working of divine and human things,
" liberty begets liberty.

" Those nations alone which are gasping in
" the clutches of absolute power, are unable to
" do anything to breathe freely ; since the very
" air is wanting to them, and the mouth of their
" masters is fastened upon theirs with a seal of
" brass.

" Such was not the position of France. She
" had her Charta, independent assemblies, a free
" press, writers, orators, a religion to which her
" soul clung; and when a people is thus armed,
" it is its own fault if it does not conquer the
" lawful rights which are still wanting to it."*

We may say, that, in this eloquent review
of the great victory which immortalized his name,
Lacordaire has not done himself justice. He
has not sufficiently said how, without his well-
known and undisputed liberalism, without his
resolute attachment to the principles of modern
society, he never could have seen the success
of his *Memorial for the re-establishment of the
Friars-Preachers*, he would never have been
listened to by the mass, nor would he ever have
gained over public opinion the cause of the religious orders. And let us not forget it; he had
gained this cause openly; and not only the cause
of his own order, which was thought to be for

---

* Memoir, dictated in October, 1861.

ever crushed by the unpopularity of the Inquisition, but the cause of all religious institutes,
even that of the Jesuits. The latter had for a
moment been menaced by a famous " order of
" the day,"* and for a moment apparently dispersed by order of their general.

But anti-monastic hatred had not ventured
further. Why? Because Father Lacordaire had
dared to appear in his habit in Notre-Dame, and
claiming boldly and honestly the liberty of conscience proclaimed in 1789, had put on his side
that floating mass, which, in all countries and in
all ages, has decided all questions.

The wolves were still wolves, and we see
this plainly to-day; but Father Lacordaire had
shamed those who howled with them, and, in the
name of liberty, had turned them against the
men of oppression.

---

* Proposed by M. Thiers in the House of Deputies, in
May, 1845, and which insisted on the strict execution of the
Napoleonic decrees against religious communities.—[*Trans-
lator's Note.*]

CHAPTER VI.

PECULIARITIES OF HIS ELOQUENCE.

FROM the decisive year which inaugurated these memorable and fruitful struggles, the life of Lacordaire was divided between the cloister and the pulpit.

I am not expected to give his religious life. It is for his friars, his sons, for those whom, by an excess of love and courage, he brought forth to the religious life, in an age when everything seemed to go against such an undertaking; it is for them alone to unveil the pious mysteries of those twenty-two years spent in the rigorous and perfect observance of a rule as severe as it is detailed. I feel myself both unworthy and incapable of handling this holy theme. I will however say, and that without fear of contradiction, that no religious was ever more faithful to his state of life, waged a more cruel war against his flesh, or quenched more generously that thirst for sacrifice, which he called the "generous half of love." What the modern regenerator of the Dominican order has told us of the humiliations and penances which St. Dominic laid upon himself in order to beat down the evil propensities of nature, he himself accomplished with the energetic single-mindedness which never altered the habitually indulgent nature of his soul, nor even disturbed the serenity of his look.

The opinion is very common among those who watched him most narrowly during his monastic life, that his days were shortened by the excessive rigors of his penance.

When all the secrets of that generous life are known, the orator will pale before the religious, and the power of that voice which has moved, enlightened, and converted such multitudes of souls, will appear a less wonder than the formidable austerity of his life, the severity with which he chastised his flesh, and his passionate tenderness for Jesus Christ.

It is more my province to speak of his life as an orator. But here again Jesus Christ is the first object of my admiration and adoration. And I desire, as I ought, to insist upon this point, for fear my lay instincts, my personal leanings, my political ardour, in a narrative which will naturally catch their colour, may throw too earthly a veil over this sovereign truth. Lacordaire was above all, the priest, the confessor, the penitent disciple of Jesus crucified. Whilst yet a seminarist he had written, " I wish to put " off this natural life, and consecrate myself en- " tirely to the service of Him who will never be " either jealous, ungrateful, or base."*

Everything, too, in his words, as in his life, is stamped with that love, after which no other love is possible. Listen to that cry of super-natural tenderness which escaped him, when, at

---

* *Letter to M. Lorain*, p. 837.

the commencement of his station of 1846, on the
morrow of the fiercest of all those struggles
above mentioned, he announced his intention of
speaking on the familiar life of Jesus Christ.

"Lord Jesus; during the ten years that I
"have been preaching to this audience, Thou
"wert ever at the bottom of my discourses; but
"to-day, at last, I come more directly to Thy-
"self, to that divine face which is daily the object
"of my contemplation, to those sacred feet which
"I have so often kissed; to those loving hands
"which have so often blessed me; to that life
"whose fragrance I have inhaled from my cradle,
"which my boyhood denied, which my youth
"again learned to love, and which my manhood
"adores and preaches to every creature. O
"Father! O Master! O Lover! O Jesus! help
"me more than ever, since being nearer to Thee,
"my audience must feel it, and I must draw
"from my heart accents indicative of thy ad-
"mirable proximity."*

---

* First Conference of 1846.

The eight sermons of this year, 1846, turn exclusively upon Jesus Christ; and it is here, in my opinion, that are to be found the most marvellous treasures of his eloquence. We may judge of it by those words which one scarcely dares quote, when one has at one's service but a profane pen, but which will never be forgotten by those who had the happiness to hear them.

" In pursuit of love all our lives, we never " obtain it but in an imperfect manner, which " makes our heart bleed. And, supposing we " did obtain it during our life, what remains of " it after our death ? Granted that the prayer " of our friend follows us beyond the tomb, a " pious memory whispers our name, but in a " moment heaven and earth have gone a step " forward, oblivion descends, silence covers us, " from no quarter is ever again wafted across " our tomb the ethereal breath of love. It is " gone, for ever gone, and such is the history of " man's love.

" I am wrong, my brethren, there is a man " whose love outlives the grave : there is a man " whose sepulchre is not only glorious, as one

L

" of the prophets exclaimed, but whose sepulchre
" is loved. There is a man whose ashes, after
" the lapse of eighteen centuries, have not grown
" cold : who is daily born again in the memory
" of a countless multitude of men : who is visited
" in his cradle by shepherds, and kings bearing
" gold and incense and myrrh. There is a man
" whose footsteps are taken up by a large por-
" tion of humanity which never tires, and who,
" although he has disappeared, is followed by
" that crowd through all the sites of his ancient
" pilgrimage, upon the knees of his mother, along
" the shores of the lakes, on the mountain tops,
" along the paths of the valleys, under the dark
" shade of the olive, in the solitude of the desert.

" There is a man, dead and buried, whose
" sleeping and waking are watched, whose every
" word still vibrates, and produces more than
" love ; virtues bearing fruit in love. There is a
" man who has been nailed for centuries to a
" gibbet, and thousands of adorers daily take him
" down from the throne of his agony, cast them-
" selves on their knees before him, prostrate
" themselves in his presence, and there, stretched

" upon the ground, kiss his bleeding feet with
" unspeakable ardour. There is a man scourged,
" killed, crucified, whom an unutterable passion
" raises from death and infamy to the glory of
" a never-dying love, which finds in him peace,
" honour, joy, yea, ecstasy. There is a man
" pursued even to his tomb by undying hatred,
" and who, requiring from each successive gene-
" ration apostles and martyrs, sees apostles and
" martyrs stand forth in his service. There is
" a man, in fine, the only one whose love ever
" lasted upon earth, and thou, O Jesus, art this
" man ; thou who in thy love didst deign to
" baptize me, to anoint me, to consecrate me,
" and the very sound of whose name opens at
" this moment the depths of my soul, and snatches
" from me these accents which trouble and sur-
" prise even myself."*

Such accents might well indeed surprise him,
as they did us ; no one of us had ever heard the

---

* Thirty-ninth Conference. On the Establishment of the
Reign of Jesus Christ.

like, and of those who that day heard them,
none will ever forget them. However great their
weakness, they will never forget those days when
the chord of the beautiful, the true, the great,
and the good vibrated in their hearts under the
might of that voice; those days in which they
saw bursting forth from a sacerdotal breast, as
from the rock struck by the divine rod, that
impetuous crystal stream, surging and irresistible
as an Alpine torrent. Ah! I confidently call
around this great and cherished memory all those
whom I once saw swelling those serried ranks,
quivering with emotion around the pulpit of
Notre-Dame. They are getting scarce and old.
But without a doubt, their heart and memory
are not dead! Let them speak then, and tell all
the blameless happiness, the holy fire, the invincible trust, the Christian loftiness they once owed
to the empire of that voice for ever hushed! Where
is the man from among his former hearers who
could to-day enter, sad and solitary, the silent
precincts of Notre-Dame, stop before that pulpit,
for ever widowed of its most illustrious occupant,
without hearing within him the echo of that peer-

less voice, without seeing with the eyes of his youth those spacious aisles again filled with that moved and quivering crowd, eagerly slaking their thirst at the swelling fountains of enthusiasm and faith?

" Si hi tacuerint, lapides clamabunt."

Yes, this venerable pile, which has seen so much ignominy and so much glory, will for ever guard the memory of him who brought back within its deserted walls crowds of fascinated believers, and of dazzled or converted unbelievers.

Irresistible empire of eloquence! wielded only by the greatest among the children of men, and joyfully yielded to by the most obscure, which it is right to recognize and necessary to proclaim; since in the land of Bossuet and Berryer a religious and political school has been found to curse liberty of speech, to look upon it as a public peril, and a social weakness!* "There are words,"

---

* This alludes to the invectives directed by M. Veuillot and the *Univers* against all public speakers in all free countries. —[*Translator's Note.*]

said Madame Swetchine, "which are equal to the "best of actions, since they contain them all in "the germ, and when the look and the accent "are true to them, it is no longer earth, it is "a revelation of the infinite."*

It is precisely this look and this accent (of which Lacordaire, more so than any other, held the secret) which constitute the charm and price of eloquence, and which give the spoken so vast a superiority over the written word.

Why is Cicero, among the ancients, and Bossuet among moderns—men who spoke much more than they wrote—especially renowned as orators? How is it that Demosthenes, Pericles, Chatham, Burke, and Mirabeau excite, after the lapse of a century, or of twenty centuries, unrivalled admiration? It is because man requires to hear, to see him who preaches to him justice and truth. The multitude, and posterity itself who have never seen nor heard the orator, require to know that on

* *Pensées*, vol. i., 811.

a given day, he stood face to face with his fellows, that he exchanged glances with them, defied their murmurs, or commanded their silence. They require to know that on his brow and in his attitude everything corresponded with his words; to know that he was not one of those ambiguous creatures who know how to coin in some secret recess, without emotion and without peril, their homilies or their imprecations. This is the touchstone of sincerity and courage, the secret of that supreme empire and that great gift of eloquence, which is the despair of all those low-born scribes who never open their mouth in public; which excites their bitterest spleen, and makes them repeat like the Athenians—when slaves of the Cæsars and rebels to the preaching of St. Paul: *Quid vult seminiverbius hic ?* This it is which prevents every comer from winning and holding empire over souls. This it is which converts the human voice into so exquisite and heavenly a music, when enlisted in the service of truth, tenderness, and courage.

But who will give us the lightning of that look of Lacordaire, the power of that action which

" completes speech ?" Who will depict those surprises, those bold flights, those familiarities, in which seemed to delight a genius always as bold as it was sure, edging along the precipice without ever falling into it; then darting upwards into the clouds with a flight that Bossuet alone has surpassed in the French pulpit, which literally carried away his audience, and left it a prey to an emotion which only one word can pourtray— the word *rapture*—of which so vulgar an abuse is made, but which, in Christian language, reminds us of the miraculous visions of St. Paul : *Quoniam raptus est in Paradisum !*

Yes, like St. Paul, and his own two glorious countrymen, St. Bernard and Bossuet, this little Burgundian priest of our own day and country was a real prince of eloquence : *Quoniam ipse erat dux verbi.**

He knew the way to our hearts ; he carried

---

* Acts xiv. 2.

and captivated them ; not by that ephemeral and commonplace admiration evoked by talent, but by that mysterious empire given to human speech when it draws its power from on high, and becomes that sacerdotal eloquence which Lacordaire carried to perfection, the secret of which he fully possessed, and the nature of which he has himself thus defined :

" The priest is an eloquent man, since he is
" set up to give living accents to the word of God,
" and eloquence is nothing other than the living
" word. The priest holds in his hands two shrines,
" the Scriptures and the tabernacle of the altar ;
" both contain under inanimate signs the eternal
" life ; both wait to be opened to the multitude
" craving for the bread of the word and the
" bread of life. How could the priest, possessed
" of this double treasure, and believing in them
" from his inmost soul, be other than eloquent ?

" All saints are eloquent—eloquent without
" genius ; since if genius be a necessary condition
" of human, it is not so of divine, eloquence.
" Faith and love can do without genius : they

" speak, and the whole earth yields to their
" sway."*

But is it true that the prodigious effect produced by the eloquence of Lacordaire was owing
solely to extemporization? Will nothing of it
remain "after those short years of the orator, and
" those ephemeral assemblies that flock around
" the voice of a man, and are then dispersed
" for ever ?"† Can we admit, with a critic
sometimes happier in his appreciations, that
Lacordaire's sermons " are to-day unreadable,
" and that their publication, by doing away with
" the brilliant lava of extemporization, has left us
" nothing but a mass of dross ?"‡

Were we to give vent to a similar opinion upon
some Protestant orator, we should certainly be
charged with sacrificing truth to sectarian spirit.
I prefer the supposition that the originator of this
strange judgment has never opened the four

---

* *Panegyric of the B. Peter Fourier.*
† *Notice on Frédéric Ozanam.*
‡ M. Ed. Scherer, in the *Temps* of 8th December, 1861.

volumes which contain the sermons of the illustrious deceased; and I am confident that of all
those who have read them not one will accept this
judgment.

Much of Lacordaire's success was undoubtedly
due to improvisation ; for he was, what is a very
rare thing, a real extempore speaker! He prepared his discourses by short but intense labour,
and did not write them.   He corrected but slightly,
I may say, too slightly, the short-hand copy of
each of his conferences, taken beneath the pulpit,
handed over to his examination the following
day, and published during the week in the form
in which they have ever since appeared.

There was doubtless in his accent, almost in
the same degree as in M. Berryer's, (that other
monarch of extempore speakers,) that piercing and
inimitable something which strikes the very deepest
chords of the soul, and which, whilst it testifies to
the reality and depth of the orator's emotion,
carries away and captivates the hearer.   I still
remember, with an inward shudder, the despairing
ring of his voice, when, in the picture drawn by
him of the frailty of human love, quoted a few

pages back, he uttered the words : " It is gone,
" for ever gone !"

But I do not hesitate to affirm, setting aside all
the partiality of a friend, and relying on a certain
practical knowledge of the chief orators of my
time, that there has never been among us one
whose improvisation so well stands the test of
reading, and keeps in that crucible so much fire,
life, and freshness. Those who have heard him
and now read him, easily experience again the
same invincible charm as when they heard him.

Those who have never heard him will discover
in him, despite all his blemishes, an accomplished
writer and a wonderful orator.

That there were gaps and defects in his talent
I shall not attempt to deny. I too frequently
pointed them out to him during his lifetime not to
have a right to recognize them to-day. He was
incomplete, like all men, even the greatest. He
did not always escape the emphatic ; he did not
avoid with sufficient care declamation, and he is
responsible for the propagation of these faults
among his far too numerous imitators. His
dialectics were sometimes weak and hazy ; he

sometimes troubled and pained his hearers by giving to the objections he purposed to combat, a strength which his refutations did not always neutralize. He too seldom attained beauty by simplicity. Although his voice was undoubtedly the most eloquent that has been heard in the pulpit since the time of Bossuet, he wanted precisely that sublime simplicity by which that *incomparable* genius verges on perfection. Lacordaire had a certain leaning for subtility, not only in his expression, but also in his thought; and this was another bond between him and that noble woman whose name will stand by his in history, as it does in the heart of all those who have loved them.

No one either followed him, in the pulpit, with more tender solicitude than Madame Swetchine. " I go through," she said, "all his perils, I tremble " at every rock, I feel every stroke." And she described as well as defended this original eloquence in the following lines: " His way of " speaking acts upon the human soul in the same " way as sanctity; it wounds but it enraptures. " Never has anyone so far imperilled the cause

" to be defended, and never has anyone drawn
" more divine rays from it." *

His literary as well as his historical acquirements wanted, I will venture to say, both sureness and breadth. He had not, any more than
M. de la Mennais, seriously studied history,
especially that of the middle ages ; he had not
shared in the great renovation of historical study,
which is one of the characteristic features and
greatest glories of our century. One would have
said that his erudition was confined to the *De
Viris* and *Cornelius Nepos* on the one hand, and
on the other to the purely scholar classics, which
he had learnt by heart in his childhood. This
hair-brained Romantique, as he was believed to

---

* Letters published by M. de Falloux, vol. ii., p. 386. As
long as her health allowed her, she assisted at the conferences
of Notre-Dame. " Should you like to see the preacher's
" mother?" was asked of two persons who were listening in
evident admiration. " Why, she died ten years ago !" " No,
" there she is, look at her." And the speaker pointed to
Madame Swetchine, hidden behind a pillar ; but whose constant assiduity, vigilant attention, and manifest happiness, gave
rise to this touching mistake.

be, and termed by many, was, on the contrary, the most stubborn, and, I will add, the most narrowly stubborn of *classicals*.*

Mythology and Grecian and Roman history seemed to him an inexhaustible armoury. Never, at least in our times, was greater use and abuse made of Brutus, Socrates, Epaminondas, and Scipio. He had got together a small literary stock, with which he never parted, which he sometimes turned to wonderful account, but which frequently he did not use with sufficient sobriety.

His taste, so great and elevated, was not irreproachable : he frequently admired and quoted second-rate authors ; and not long ago he entered into a long dispute, by letter and *viva voce,* to preserve in one of his finest productions, two wretched lines from *Tancrède.* It was impossible to get him to understand that when a man wants

---

* This alludes to the quarrel between the two literary schools, termed *Les Classiques* and *Les Romantiques,* which was at its height under Charles X. and Louis Philippe, in the flourishing days of Lamartine, Victor Hugo, Alfred de Musset, &c.

to quote Voltaire, he must look somewhere else than in his tragedies. He one day said in the pulpit, " By the grace of God I have a horror " for what is commonplace," and he was never more mistaken in his life.

Not that he did not endeavour, and successfully, to avoid it in the general plan of his discourses ; but he fell into it more frequently than he imagined, in the execution. Moreover, if he did not hate commonplace, he sometimes created it ; a thing not given to everybody, which betrays a happy facility for mastering the imagination of one's contemporaries, and turning their prejudices to account.

It was he who first unearthed, in an article of the *Avenir*, that heading of the mediæval chronicle, " *Gesta Dei per Francos*," which has since been used on every possible opportunity, and on every subject in ecclesiastical literature. It was he especially who, by repeatedly bringing in the Emperor Napoleon I. and his pretended conversion at St. Helena, has made of the imperial meteor one of the most repulsive and ill-chosen common-places of the Christian pulpit.

The rightful claims of criticism having thus been satisfied with impartial severity; and all these blemishes, and many others if need be, pointed out and acknowledged, I believe I shall not be going too far if I ask whether, among the authors and writers of our day, there is a single one who will leave behind him pages superior, either in point of thought or style, to certain pages of Father Lacordaire? I must again establish this assertion by proofs, and after having quoted so much, I must be allowed to quote again, were it only this page, so new and so consoling, which one need often peruse in an age when every progress ends by facilitating and popularising despotism :

"For a long time the last of captains had held " destiny in his grasp: the Alps and Pyrenees " had trembled under him : Europe was listening " in silence to the thunder of his thought; when, " tired of the sphere in which glory had spent " itself to please him, he threw himself on to " the confines of Asia. There his eye became " troubled, and his eagles turned back for the " first time. What had he met with? A general

M

" superior to himself ? No. A yet unvanquished
" army ? No. Was age laying its icy hand on
" his genius ? No. What had he then met with ?
" He had met with the protector of the weak, the
" refuge of the oppressed, the great defender of
" human liberty; he had met with space, and all
" his power had crumbled beneath his feet.

" If God has created such barriers in the very
" bosom of nature, it is because He has had
" compassion on us. He knew all that forced
" unity involved of despotism and of disaster for
" the human race, and He prepared for us, in the
" mountains and deserts, inaccessible retreats.
" He hollowed out the rock of St. Anthony and
" St. Paul the first hermit; He made nests to
" which the eagle would not come to tear away
" the little ones of the dove. O inaccessible
" mountains, eternal snows, burning sands, nox-
" ious marshes, destructive climates, we thank
" you for the past, and we trust to you for the
" future. Yes, you will keep for us free oases,
" solitary Thebaids, trackless routes; you will
" ever protect us against the mighty of this
" world; you will not allow chemistry to prevail

" against nature, and to convert the globe, so well
" studded by the hand of God, into a horrible
" and narrow dungeon, where nothing but steam
" will be breathed in freedom, and where fire and
" sword will be the first minions of a merciless
" autocracy."*

But let us leave these questions of history
and social philosophy, to the discussion of which
our friend was perhaps too much addicted; let
us follow him into the discussion of the mysteries
of the soul, which he has traversed, probed, and
described with such moving perspicacity.

Where can we find a more masterly and
sweeter picture of that pure and generous melancholy aroused in the soul of youth by the thirst
after the infinite ? Is not the pen of Réné,
purified and nerved by supreme truth, visible
in the following lines ?

" Scarcely do we count eighteen summers
" when we languish with desires, whose object

------

* Conferences of Notre-Dame, Thirty-first Conference, 1845.

" is neither the flesh, nor love, nor glory, nor
" anything that has a shape or a name. Wander-
" ing in the silence of solitude, or in the splendid
" thoroughfares of great cities, the young man
" feels oppressed with yearnings that have no
" aim ; he flies the realities of life as a prison
" in which his heart is stifled, and he seeks in
" everything that is uncertain and vague, in the
" evening cloud, in the breeze of autumn, in the
" falling leaves of the woods, an impression
" which fills whilst it tortures him.

" But it is in vain ; the clouds fleet by, the
" winds are hushed, the leaves fade and wither
" without telling him why he suffers, without
" sating his soul, any more than the tears of a
" mother, or the tender affection of a sister. O
" soul! would the prophet exclaim, why art thou
" sad, why art thou troubled ? Trust in God. It
" is, in fact, God ; it is the infinite which is at
" work in our hearts of twenty years, touched by
" Christ, but which have unwittingly strayed from
" him, and in which the divine unction, no longer
" producing its supernatural effect, still wakes up
" the storms it was destined to calm. Even in old

" age we receive some of these shocks of bygone
" days—some of those melancholy day-dreams
" which the ancients looked upon as the portion of
" genius, and which gave rise to the saying : ' *Non*
" ' *est magnum ingenium sine melancholia.*' The
" soul, faltering betimes, returns in pain within
" herself ; she betakes herself to the days of her
" youth, to seek for her tears, and no longer able
" to weep as of old, she lives for a moment
" upon the painful but sweet memory of those
" tears."*

He who spoke thus ten years before his death,
had without doubt gone through these sweet and
perilous reveries.   But how are we to account for
the depth and truthfulness of the accents in which
he depicted emotions he had never known ?   Whilst
still young, he answered a friend who had informed
him of his marriage : " I too hope to marry some
" day.   I have a betrothed, lovely, chaste, and
" immortal ; and our marriage, celebrated on earth,

---

* Sixtieth Conference, 1850.

" will be consummated in heaven. I shall never
" say : *Linquenda domus et placens uxor.*"*

Upon his death-bed he said, " Before loving
" God, I loved glory, *and loved nothing else.*"

Everything within the memory of those who
best knew him proves the sincerity of this state-
ment. And yet with that marvellous penetration,
to be met with in all the great masters of
Christian eloquence, even in the cold Bourdaloue,
he explored and lighted up not only those guilty
passions, whose dark horrors stricken and penitent
consciences could lay open to him, but even more
so the mysterious recesses of those pure and lawful affections which he had renounced. He
has spoken of them with a charm in which beauty
and truthfulness go hand in hand. I extract, not
from his immortal discourse upon *Chastity*, but
from a more recent and less known one, the
following page upon love in marriage :

" If struck with compassion for your secret

---

* Letter quoted by M. Lorain, *Correspondant*, vol. xviii.,
p. 835.

" wounds, I wanted to persuade you to be chaste.
" . . . . . If some young soul aroused the tender-
" ness of my heart, and I wanted to snatch from his
" hands the deceitful cup of evil, I should say to
" him :—My friend, child of thy mother, and
" brother of thy sister—child of thy mother who
" bore thee in the sacred continence of marriage,
" brother of thy sister, of whose virtue thou art
" the witness and guardian, ah ! do not dishonour
" in thy person the great privilege of thy man-
" hood ; keep in a frail flesh the honour of thy
" soul, the religious fount whence life springs, and
" where love blossoms. Prepare for thy future
" couch holy friendship, and embraces which
" heaven and earth may bless ; be chaste if thou
" wilt love long, if thou wilt be loved for ever.

" There exists in the world, between thy mo-
" ther and thy sister, between thy forefathers and
" thy posterity, a tender and gentle creature des-
" tined by God to be thine. Hidden from every
" eye, she is practising in silence that fidelity which
" she will promise thee ; she is already living for
" thee who art unknown to her ; she is sacrificing
" for thee her inclinations, she is correcting in

" herself whatever might one day cross the slight-
" est of thy desires.　Ah! keep thy heart for her
" as she is keeping hers for thee; do not offer her
" a ruin in exchange for her youth; and since she
" is sacrificing herself for thee by an anticipation
" of love, offer up to this same love, in the *deepest*
" *recesses* of thy passions, a just and costly sacri-
" fice."*

Even in the last outpourings of his eloquence
and of his sacerdotal soul, we find this finished paint-
ing of what Pascal termed " *the passions of love.*"

" When I have said to a man, I esteem you......
" I admire you........ I venerate you : is there
" nothing else I can say to him?　Have I ex-
" hausted human language ?　No, there is still one
" thing I can say to him, only one, the last of all ;
" I can say to him : I love you.　Ten thousand
" expressions may precede that one, but after that
" no language has any other ; but one alternative
" remains, it is to repeat it to him for ever."†

---

* Sixty-first Conference.　On Trial; 1850.
† Fourth Conference of Toulouse, 1854.

"Sooner or later," says Vauvenargues, "the
"pleasures of the soul alone charm us.   But by
"reason of our constitution, partly spiritual,
"partly corporal, our first quest after souls is
"in the mirror of our being, sensible beauty.
".............. In presence of the human
"countenance, where begins the revelation of
"the invisible world, man becomes troubled. ...
"........... Even supposing he would not
"have shed a drop of blood for the universe,
"he is ready to give his whole self for a creature
"of a day, whose beauty lasts but an hour.
"A look decides him, and if suddenly speech
"be added to the look; if this power, which in
"the rest of nature is but a sound, a breath, a
"murmur, a melody, becomes a living voice which
"speaks the language of the soul, then love, which
"was but an instinct, is itself transformed with
"the beauty which awoke it, and death itself
"is powerless against a feeling which can be
"mastered only by virtue.   Alas! I am wrong.
"Time too is master of it.   The fruit of the
"senses more so than of the mind, this love de-
"pends upon the breath that crosses the face of

" the beloved. A change of feature, a wrinkle,
" will blight it. Often, even when the cause re-
" mains, the effect vanishes. Unbounded love is
" seen betimes to fall like a wind that subsides,
" and he who a few moments ago adored, knows
" not whence comes the indifference that has
" frozen his transports........... Love then,
" like everything lasting, requires the ocean of
" eternity.......... But can we ever love God
" heart to heart, like a living being which we hold
" in our embrace, which speaks to us, answers us,
" and says, I love you? Ah! doubtless this word
" is a deception in the mouth of man; love is fre-
" quently betrayed, more frequently forgotten, but
" still it is professed, professed sincerely, professed
" with the conviction that it will never be with-
" drawn. It fills with its immensity one day of
" our existence, and when it falls to the ground
" like a faded flower, we still give it a share in
" our thoughts, a sweet and hallowed shrine."

Let us show this priest battling with the
transports and miscalculations of human ties, and
let us see how he manages to lead gently to the
divine refuge a heart intoxicated and wounded by

the chimeras of the passions. Let us borrow from his letters, more eloquent if possible than his discourses, this fragment put at our disposal with confiding generosity, and which, whilst still young, he addressed to a friend young like himself, whom sorrow of heart had induced to seek for a few days' retreat in a community.

" God has given you a weighty share of the
" trials of this life ; He has stricken you as though
" wilfully, less like a child one chastises than
" as a victim one immolates, and still you do
" not seem to see the bent He has given you for
" Himself. If He wishes to possess your whole
" soul, can we be surprised that He deprives it of
" everything capable of leading it astray ? The
" Gospel tells us He is a kind God. Those
" caresses of which you dream, that sweet and
" lawful love which would overflow like a balm
" from your stricken heart ; those ineffable de-
" lights of pure affection of which men are allowed
" to get a snatch ; why should not your Lord be
" afraid that these things would prevent you from
" loving Him alone ? ' *We have been crushed, in*
" ' *order to our fusion,*' said M. de Maistre, of the

" peoples of Europe.   When God crushes us under
" the rod, is it not with a view that our blood may
" mingle with his, with his shed long ago under
" harder and more humiliating strokes ?   Is it not
" that we may seek no other face than the bleed-
" ing face of our Saviour, no other eyes than
" his, no other lips than his, no other shoulders
" than his shoulders torn by the scourge, no
" other hands and feet to kiss than his hands
" and feet pierced with nails for love of us, no
" other wounds to tend with gentleness than his
" divine and ever bleeding wounds ?   Ah ! my
" friend, is not love ever love ?   You complain
" that you are not loved, and God has given you
" in the bottom of your heart a chaste, immense,
" invincible love.   You would fain harbour an-
" other profane love, and God, who perhaps
" does not will it, strikes and wounds you ; He
" shows you the infinite, the vanity of the world ;
" He crucifies you in order to get you to love
" his crucified Son more, and realize that cruci-
" fixion in yourself.   You will probably get my
" letter in solitude, in a place where there are
" others too who could have loved the creature

" with rapture, and they have sacrificed it to God.
" I do not know his special designs in your regard,
" but I know that his design upon all men is to be
" loved by them, and that the whole conduct of
" his providence is directed to this end."

Thus it was that Lacordaire spoke to young
men of that youthful love which he had never
known. And, what is perhaps more wonderful,
he has sounded quite as well, without ever having
felt it, another love, the purest and most ardent,
the most tender and lawful of all. Last in the
order of time, it outdoes and outlives everything ;
it feeds on everything that disappears around us,
and grows strong on everything that casts us
down ; it pierces the heart, grown tender in its
loneliness, with a keener and more penetrating
shaft than do the most fervid passions of youth.

It is the passion of the father for the child,
especially of the father or grandfather, as life
begins to wane, for the blessed young soul which
is growing up under his eyes. How could it be
otherwise ? Neither the first fires of the dawn,
nor the spring in its first freshness, nor the rose
in its first fragrance, nor the first song of the

nightingale on an April or May night, no, nothing, nothing at all in nature or art equals the beauty, the purity, the peerless grace of the child. And nothing, even in religion itself, draws towards God, reveals God, like the faith and candour of the child, like its heart, its voice, its look: that heart so guileless and so eager, which wants to get everything, because it gives its whole self, and to know everything, because it has nothing to hide : that voice so full of sweet and artless music, which speaks to man as man should always speak to God: that calm, mild, bright and open look which dives without an effort into the secrets of heaven!

Their angels always see the face of God. " They themselves are unconscious of it; but they " live and bound with joy in this light, in which " they grow, full of hopes, germs, and ravishing " feelings."*

Those who love them and live no longer on

---

* *Le P. Gratry. Les Sources*, Part II.

any but this love, are betimes bathed in this
heavenly light.   The wisdom of nations has said,
" *Did Youth but know!   If Age but could!* "
Now the father who loves, the old father, has
at the same time the knowledge and power ; he
knows he can love without bounds, as well as
without reproach.............   I forbear for
fear these lines may perchance pierce some heart
stricken at not having known this happiness, or
having known it, at having lost it for ever.

But even in this supreme and spotless joy, as
in everything else, the bitterness, the weakness
inseparable from human things, crop out.   Lacordaire thus breaks it to us, explains it, and com-
forts us :

" With the first shades of age the feeling of
" paternity descends upon our soul, and fills up
" the void left by previous affection.

" Do not imagine that this is a falling-off;
" next to the look of God upon the world, nothing
" is more beautiful than the look of the old man
" upon the child; a look so pure, so tender, so
" unselfish; one which marks in our life the culmi-
" nating point of perfection, and the closest like-

" ness with God. The body bends with age, the
" mind too perchance, but not the soul by which
" we love. Paternity is as much above love as
" love is above friendship. It would be full and
" spotless love, if the return made by the child
" to the father were the return of the friend to
" the friend, of the husband to the spouse;
" but such is not the case.

    " When children, the love we returned was
" unequal to the love received; and now that we
" are old in our turn, we love more than we are
" loved. We must not complain.

    " Your children follow in your wake, the
" wake of friendship, the wake of love, burning
" paths, which do not allow them to requite that
" hoary passion called paternity. Man finds in
" his children the same powerlessness to requite
" his love as he himself experienced when a child,
" and has thus the honor to end in a disin-
" terested love like that of God."*

    One does not tire of copying such pages.

---

* Conferences of Notre-Dame, Thirty-ninth Conference, 1840.

And still, if we are to believe the arrogant disdain of infidel criticism, Father Lacordaire has not left "in all his oratorical works a single " passage which may be called eloquent, a sin- " gle phrase which still touches a fibre of our " hearts."*

---

* M. Ed. Scherer, *Le Temps*, 8th December, 1861.

CHAPTER VII.

ERRONEOUS JUDGMENTS OF WHICH HE WAS THE
OBJECT.—HIS CHARACTER AND HIS QUALITIES.

But we have spoken at too great length of
the orator: let us examine the man.   Let us see
whether, in his public, as well as his private
capacity, there is not more than one side of his
character altogether unknown, which requires to
be thrown into relief; and whether there is not
more than one singular mistake about him to be
rectified.   Let us see him tried by renown, by the
great position which he won, by his passionate
admirers as well as by his stubborn detractors.

When he had entered upon the possession of
glory, (for the word may be well applied to the

immense popularity he long enjoyed,) he never appeared dazzled by it: he preserved, in all the glory of his triumphs, the modesty and simplicity of a child. He seems to have seen himself as in a mirror, when he spoke of his friend Ozanam in the following terms, " That coveted goal of " lasting success, which is nearly always the " signal for a selfish change in the heart of man, " left him as it found him.......... During " the twenty years that I have known him, I " have frequently seen him troubled and indig- " nant, without ever having been able to discover " in him even the shadow of haughtiness or af- " fectation, and this is the evident mark of a " soul superior to fortune, and constantly intent · " upon God alone."

Great in triumph, he was greater still in the contest with that hatred and envy which never ceased to follow him.

Really great men are nearly always ill-judged and misunderstood by their contemporaries. No one, perhaps, ever enjoyed this privilege of great- ness in the same degree as Lacordaire.

Whoever is acquainted with his life and his

soul, must remain astounded at the falseness and stupidity of a crowd of judgments passed upon him. For he had not only, like every superior man, to contend with jealousy, ignorance, and frivolity; and moreover like all public men in this country, with the wretched fickleness of the French character; but he encountered, besides, a special class of adversaries, in all those who were annoyed at the rare nobleness of his character, as well as at the striking originality of his talent. Having reached the climax of his powers and renown, at a time especially remarkable for the quick-spreading decline of character and convictions, for the sudden and complete fall of the moral temperature of the country, he bitterly galled all those to whom his intrepid sadness was a standing reproach.

His high and pure soul, incapable of running after fortune, in no matter what shape, appeared to blame too severely all those who had not imitated him. The blind and childish hostility which had assailed him from the outset, grew in intensity during the latter years of his life. The distrust which the bold originality of his first manner was calculated to awaken, had subsided in all right-minded men, before the *ensemble* of his career, and the final wisdom of his line of conduct: but in the common leaven this distrust had been succeeded by a sort of repulsion tinged with terror.

The little-minded and small-hearted, incapable of enthusiasm, courage, and generosity, unable to understand strength of will in action, and dignity in retreat, had ever misunderstood and calumniated him: they followed him with their impotent dislike until his last hour. For a moment they might have supposed him crushed under the weight of events and of their glutted hostility. Such was not the case; shrouded for a time by the storm, his glory always re-appeared pure and unshaken. It described its orbit like a planet attended by satellites, not bright and obedient, but destined to enhance, by their dulness, its victorious splendour.

Thus he made his way, ever crossed, and ever triumphant, from his first conferences at the Collège Stanislas, where certain priests reproached him with never having pronounced the name of Jesus Christ, until that glorious epilogue of his

whole life, that speech on his reception at the
Academy, so lofty, so noble, so Christian; and
in which, for want of other grievances, his pious
detractors discovered a crime in the mere fact of
his having quoted *Montesquieu.*

Without ever closing his eyes to the hostility
of which he was the butt, he always met it
with simple dignity and serene indifference. No
one knew it better, nor treated it with colder
disdain. No one ever surprised upon his lips
a bitter word against his denouncers and his
persecutors. He met the meannesses of jealousy, as
well as the most threatening storms, with the same
arm—silence. " When a man puts a mile between
" himself and me, I put ten thousand between
" myself and him, and think no more about it."*

"I felt," said he, in speaking of the station†
which made him master of Paris in 1836, "I

---

* 10th August, 1840.
    † This word has a peculiar meaning in France. It is used
to designate a series of sermons given usually by the same
preacher, from the first Sunday of Advent until the Epiphany;
and from the first Sunday of Lent until Low Sunday. These
two periods are called *Stations.*

" felt everywhere around me a concentrated fury
" which was seeking in every direction an outlet
" for its ill-will. Even were the Pope to shield
" me with his hand during the whole of my life,
" still I should not escape a single insult, a single
" calumny, a single innuendo of grovelling suspicion.
" All that I have to do is to be blameless at Rome
" and at Paris, to be prudent, to work under the
" protection of God with invincible energy, and
" to treat his enemies with the most rigid silence."*

As he advanced in life, the consciousness of
the enmity, of which he was the object, must
have been purified and calmed, without becoming
less poignant. "In proportion to my vocation
" in the Church, God has heaped upon me, for
" nearly twenty years, an unbroken succession
" of painful trials. From my entrance into the
" seminary in 1824, until my station of 1844
" at Paris, I was the butt of the most stubborn
" enmity of a certain number of men, able to

---

* 18th August, 1887.

" do much damage, who left no stone unturned
" to blast my reputation, and drive me to ex-
" tremities. Twenty years of patience, gentle-
" ness, and perseverance, have been the price
" of a little peace, which will last as long as
" God sees fit."*

Of all the errors which have circulated about
Lacordaire, the most generally received was that
which depicted him as a violent and passionate
mind, fond of disturbance and conflict, given especially to certain utopies, and unable to check
or restrain itself. This is precisely the reverse
of the truth.

No one had a keener eye than he for the
real, and the possible. He possessed a stock
of solid and unvarying good sense. Like a
fiery charger, trained to war, he always knew
how to obey the bit and regulate his movements.
If betimes aspirations a degree too ardent, and
unmatured conceptions, for a moment giddied, and

---

* 22nd July, 1846.

carried him away, these mists broke suddenly, and allowed him to see the real ground of things ; in a moment he drew up and turned short with the energetic precision which characterized him in everything.

He was a man of both great imagination and great good sense. Of all the rare faculties with which he was endowed, none was so fully developed as that of reflection. It rendered him capable of long designs and deep calculations. No one more carefully weighed his resolutions, or more thoroughly sifted all their consequences. Once taken, he clung to them with inflexible tenacity. What I always and chiefly remarked in him, beside other gifts, more brilliant perhaps, but not more essential, was unflinching firmness joined with heroic patience.

" I have but one political principle," he wrote, " and that is never to yield an inch ; strength is " only acquired by this invincible firmness.... "*

---

* 30th January, 1838.

" Nothing useful is ever gained by fear of
" anything but error and cowardice."*

" Whenever dignity is at stake, I look neither
" to the right nor the left, but only to what is
" honorable, trusting to Providence for the rest."†

" To accomplish duty with courage and single-
" mindedness is the surest way to obtain from
" men the justice of a real admiration."‡

" To betake oneself to one's own interior and
" to God, gives the greatest strength in the world."§

" .... I await in patience, without taking up
" my own defence, leaving to time that providential
" action which brings men back to wisdom ..."||

It may be seen that I borrow more frequent,
if not more extensive quotations from his letters
than from his discourses. Whilst they were both
still living, Madame Swetchine very frequently
said of him : " *He will be rightly known only by*
" *his letters.*" This judgment will be ratified by

---

* 8th April, 1837.   † 13th April, 1837.
‡ 15th May, 1844.   § 10th April, 1840.
               || 10th April, 1840.

all those who have preserved the text or the memory of these letters. It is in them—I fear not to affirm it—that his genius, and his soul still more lofty than his genius, will shine in their purest light. The next century will be able to enjoy, fully, those outpourings of faith, poetry, tenderness, high-mindedness, and sometimes sweet slyness which was less foreign to him than is supposed. *Scribantur hæc in generatione altera.*

There will be found even to his very handwriting, engraven as though for posterity, without correction or stain, even in the most confidential and hurried of his letters, a new proof of the marvellous faculty of improvisation with which he was gifted.

To-day certain traits only can be extracted from this treasure, calculated to aid in the appreciation of this singular and attractive character. I will quote here two passages which will show with what delicacy and elevation this priest, this religious, superior to glory, and indifferent to fortune, judged, whilst surveying them by the light of his soul, these two great tempters of human nature.

" A celebrated name ought not to be a hack-
"neyed one. Every day the names of ministers
" or members are in the public papers, whilst
" there are great names whose very glory forbids
" their frequent production. I am struck by the
" idea how little the men of our day understand
" the secret of glory ; they nearly all break down
" by puerile vanity. Glory is like beauty ; it is
" heightened by modesty."*

He added later on, when speaking of a great but
fallen mind : " Poor man ! he adds another to the
" already numerous list of glory's apostates, and
" I admire the manner in which God withdraws
" from them the usually keen sense of pride !"†

So much for glory, which had been his first
and only passion. Now for fortune : " In general
" the great men of antiquity were poor... This
" is the rock upon which everyone splits to-
" day.. People no longer know how to live on
" little. It is true that, used as I have been to

---

* Florence, 11th August, 1838.
† Strasburg, 23rd March, 1846.

" live poor from my birth, I may be unable to
" see the difficulties in the way of those whose
" habits are not like my own. But retrenchment
" of the useless, the want even of the *relatively*
" *necessary*, is the high road to Christian self-
" denial as well as to antique strength of cha-
" racter.... Whoever has attained the moral
" beauty of life, not only before God, but before
" men, cannot give way under mere material re-
" verses without showing that his greatness of
" soul was hollow, his cleverness simply a piece
" of good luck. That of which our age stands
" most in need is a man able to gratify every desire,
" and content with little. For my part, humanly
" speaking, I ambition nothing more. A great heart
" in a little house is of all things here below that
" which has ever touched me most. The Abbé de la
" Mennais, dying poor and faithful at La Chesnaie,
" would have been the hero of this age, in which
" the fortune of every man is above his deserts."*

---

* Notre Dame de Chalais, 22nd July, 1846.

This view of real glory, this noble contempt of fortune, this "*great heart in a small house*," all this was easy to him, thanks to the height upon which the ardent simplicity of his faith, and his confidence in God, placed him.

Thus his confidence in God's justice, even in this world, in the unforeseen but inevitable triumph of truth, was boundless. He was continually studying the providential march of events, tracing it, pointing it out to others, and blessing it.

" I have always seen God justify Himself in " the long run ; I am continually discovering that " I misunderstood and murmured with Him when " He was kindest. . . . . ."*

" We must listen to the lies of our enemies " and wait for truth, which makes its way in " its own time, although slowly."†

At those periods of his life when he was most harassed, and most forsaken, when his closest

---

* 15th March, 1833.   † Rome, 21st June, 1836.

confidants gave way to sadness, through terror at the general desertion of justice and truth, he, casting his piercing glance beyond time and space, seemed to descry afar unknown multitudes, an army of still dumb but unmistakeable auxiliaries, a whole posterity of victorious and avenging followers.

" When something is to be done, it is a great " mistake to imagine that everything is not done " as soon as a good germ is produced and sown. " Happy the man that soweth the good and the " true ! the harvest will not fail him."*

" Let us work earnestly, to the best of our " power, and leave the future to dawn with that " modesty which God lends to all his works, and " which by the slowness of success, takes from " man the glory of them."†

" Provided we be humble, without party spirit, " really devoted to God alone, ready to live or " die, we shall never want, either in failure or

---

* Solesmes, 1st July, 1838.   † Les Chaises, 25th July, 1838.

" success, those consolations of the Christian who
" has done his best, and who receives everything
" God wills......."*

" It is God who raises up men, when He wants
" them, and who gives them exactly what is
" necessary, by a series of events whose con-
" nection is only discovered by lapse of time.
" From whatever point of view I look at my past
" life, I find every portion of it converging to-
" wards my present position....."†

" We shall not die before seeing another
" generation of men; God will give us before
" our death a kind of twilight glimpse of future
" men... Whatever happen, facts will stand,
" and heirs will be given us to gather in the
" harvest."‡

" I abandon myself to God; his ever bene-
" ficent hand keeps me more and more in adora-
" tion and gratitude."§... "God intended the

---

* Dijon, 4th October, 1838.
† Aisey le Duc, 2nd November, 1838.
  La Quercia, May 10th, 1839.   § Rome.

" whole of my past life to be a schooling in the
" patient endurance of injustice. . . . . . ."*

" The questions of this world are so knotty,
" they present themselves so diversely and con-
" tradictorily to different minds, that I consider
" it a great blessing when they are solved by
" events independent of the will of man. I have
" always passionately wished for this sort of solu-
" tion, even so as to be slightly superstitious about
" them."†

" Since the outset of my public life, now ten
" years ago, I have never looked anywhere but
" on high for my duty and my fate."‡

" We must believe absolutely and unhesita-
" tingly that what comes from God is best, even
" when it seems to us worst, in a human point
" of view. I have seen this exemplified twenty
" times during my life, and this experience always
" gave me an unbounded submission to the will
" of God, which is now my greatest stay, and

---

* St. Clemente, 11th May, 1841.
† Rome, 30th August, 1837.
‡ Rome, St. Sabine, 25th October, 1840.

" which aids me against all the imperfections of
" a nature hasty and inclined to carry things
" with a high hand."

But I return to the feature by which I began
this familiar portrait. From his youth upwards,
as I believe I have clearly shown by the recital
of his relations with M. de la Mennais, he possessed the art of combining sound moderation
of judgment, and rare prudence of conduct, with
the ardour of his opinions and the boldness of
his resolves. " Look," he wrote to me whilst still
quite young, " look at the story of our troubles,
" and tell me who are those whose memory has
" remained pure. Those only who were never
" extreme ; all others have forfeited the esteem of
" their country."*

Twenty years later he said, and with good
reason : " The *modus in rebus* is my most con-
" stant study, convinced as I am that moderation
" is scarcest and stoutest of all weapons."†

---

* Bosco, 4th October, 1842.
† Flavigny, 27th February, 1853.

Moderation then, *le juste milieu,* was in everything the rule of his action; and yet it never
hindered him from coming, at the right moment,
to bold decisions, with the energy peculiar to
pure and upright hearts.

A base thought never crossed that great soul
any more than a discord marred the harmony of
that great life.   In certain peculiarly delicate
circumstances, he showed a rare mixture of tact
and dignity, and I am desirous only to direct
here the attention of his future biographer to the
whole course of his relations with Mgr. de Quelen,
his first archbishop, in whose case he had sometimes as much reason to complain as to congratu-
late himself, and whose vacillation, joined to the
influence of events, ended in a separation which
allowed his illustrious client to feel himself " free
" without being ungrateful."

To these qualities, essential to the public man,
the man of business, the creator of religious foundations, were added a rare spirit of order and
method, a passion for precision, neatness, and good
arrangement, despite the extreme simplicity and
poverty of his habits.

O 2

This taste, which he preserved until his latest breath, almost degenerated into minutiousness. It was visible in his very least habits, as all those were able to testify who were admitted into that cell where he received friends, disciples, especially youths, with such effusion; but where some found nothing else to do but look with stupor into every nook, when received with that chilling silence, which no one ever carried farther than he, when he had to do with indiscreet visitors, or inquisitive guests.

This moderation and precision, which ruled his judgments and conduct, were carried by him into his religious teaching, and clung to with inviolable fidelity.

The splendour of his talent never detracted from the soundness of his doctrine. " His bril- " liancy," said an excellent judge, M. Augustin Cochin, " veiled his solidity." Under a form betimes excessive and violent, there never lay any but moderate opinions. The perfect orthodoxy of his doctrines has never been seriously assailed. Those who believed themselves entitled to question it most loudly have never been able to quote anything but garbled extracts of his discourses, frequently distorted from their real meaning.

Now isolated phrases or metaphors of questionable worth, debateable imagery, and epithets, could never be construed into errors against faith. What is quite certain is, that having treated during twenty years, both in the pulpit and in writing, the most delicate dogmatic subjects, he never incurred public censure upon any single point, or on the part of any single authority ; and his conferences, having been submitted to a consultor of the *Index*, were recognized as safe from all condemnation.*

A prince of the Church, whose courageous support is never wanting to a good cause, has rendered this public testimony, in pronouncing his funeral oration : " After the most searching " examination, out of the whole series of ques- " tions, ever profound, often undecided, discussed " by his masculine genius, no single proposition

---

* " *Irreproachable*," says his letter of the 5th of June, 1857. He adds, " This is at least what has been affirmed to me."

" has been, on the part of Rome, the object of
" censure, or even of criticism ; and that is the
" reason of my presence in this pulpit."*

" I am aware," he wrote, " that many judge me
" wrongly, and consider me the plaything of my
" ideas ; it is my form of speech which thus de-
" ceives them. It conceals the scrupulous care
" which I bring to bear upon the groundwork, and
" which has frequently delivered me from snares in
" which I might have perished. A day will come
" when the orator will give place to the theolo-
" gian ; but death must intervene. Too many
" storms have beaten my bark to allow people to
" see as yet how I have steered it !"†

This form, so new as well as brilliant, so different from the old traditions of the French
pulpit, always terrified a large number of superficial or malevolent minds. And yet what more

---

* *Funeral Oration of Father Lacordaire*, by His Eminence
Cardinal Donnet, Archbishop of Bordeaux, pronounced on the
16th of January, 1862, p. 13.
　　　　† Sorèze, 5th June, 1857.

necessary or more natural than this newness of form in the midst of a society so thoroughly new? That which he attempted, and in which he succeeded beyond any other, was to attract, to move, to reconcile to the word of the priest the hostile and indifferent crowd, and chiefly youth. As has been shown to evidence by one of those men who most love and honor contemporary society, the Viscount de Melun, his singularity and boldness have been justified by the multitude of new believers, drawn by his eloquence to the foot of the altar, the way to which they had either forgotten or never known. The very sermon which some pious person would consider rash or out of place, was precisely the one which attracted the sceptic, shook the infidel, and opened to truth their minds and hearts. We must observe, too, that the only novelty about him was in the expression, or, at the outside, in the relation which he established between the old doctrine and new requirements. Inverting the method pointed out by André Chénier,

" Sur des pensers nouveaux faisons des vers antiques,"

he wanted simply to throw upon old, immutable, eternal truths a new light, by adapting them, with all the seductions of the most original coloring, to the wants and habits of modern minds.

He never pretended to discover new truths; he never sacrificed an old truth to new ideas; but he took hold of these ideas, and made them Christian, in order to conciliate the aspirations of the day with the doctrines of the Gospel. It was no concession, it was a conquest.*

To deny that Christian apology and contro- versy ought to offer different characters according to the requirements of times and events, would be to deny to the Church the faculty of motion, that is to say, of life; and that progress of light and certitude which her greatest geniuses and most faithful children have claimed for her, from St. Vincent of Lerius to the present day.†

---

* M. de Melun.

† " Nullusne ergo in Ecclesia Christi profectus habebitur " intelligentiæ ?   Habebitur planè et maximus, sed ità tamen " ut vere profectus sit ille fidei, non permutatio."—*Commoni- torium*, c. xxix.

Lacordaire had, moreover, undertaken a task still more indispensable than novel in an age when religious dogmas are hardly discussed or studied at all, but in which the action of the Church upon society is daily calumniated, ridiculed, or denied. Himself converted to the truth by the social and historical evidences of Catholicism, he was desirous of impressing the weight of those evidences upon the souls of his contemporaries. In this task, so gloriously brought about by him, he had no pattern, no forerunner.

He has, unfortunately, had too large a number of imitators, who, relying upon his example, have flooded our pulpits with historical, political, and economical elucubrations, as superficial as questionable : to such a degree, that, after having heard them, it is a real pleasure to hear the *prône* of some modest village curé, who confines himself to commenting upon a page of the Gospel, or a page of the catechism. But Lacordaire cannot be held accountable for the aberrations of the *servum pecus* of his clumsy copiers. He himself was fitted to treat dogmatic and moral questions with as original and orthodox a solidity as social

and historical ones ; he has shown it in his conferences upon *Chastity,* upon *Jesus Christ,* and the
Supernatural Commerce of God with Man.

We can never sufficiently lament that sickness
and death stopped him at a moment when he was
entering more deeply into that field which he had
so happily opened up by his admirable *Letters to a
Young Man upon Christian Life.*

But as to the first part of his plan, it must
be acknowledged, and it was the newest and most
difficult, that he filled it up with as much talent
as fruit. Among moderns, no one has rendered
more evident the immortal union between the
teachings of religion and the fundamental laws of
honor, virtue, and justice, upon which Christian
society is based, and which Pius IX. proclaimed,
too, with such sovereign authority, in his brief to
the Archbishop of Warsaw.*

---

* " Ne desinas vero unquam .... eosdem fideles populos
" ..... semper monere, exhortari, excitare, ut a veritatis,
" honoris, virtutis, justitiæque semita, ac sanctissimis divinæ
" nostræ religionis præceptionibus nunquam deflectant."—
Brief of June 6th, 1861.

Whilst pursuing this task, which will associate his name and his work with the glorious immortality of the Church, he ever remained obedient to that spouse of Christ whose trials had moved his heart, whose teachings had subdued his proud intelligence, and in whose service he spent his life. Whilst soaring in his lofty and bold flight through the most diverse regions, whilst sailing aloft in the highest of the heavens, this eagle fixed his ever faithful and intrepid gaze upon the sun of the Church,

" Quel sol che pria d' amor *gli* scaldo 'l petto."*

I say the Church, the spouse of Jesus Christ, and not such or such opinions, passions, or fantasies, obtaining for a time among the Catholics of a given country or party. For even in the ardour of his unshaken orthodoxy I find that moderation and precision, to which I shall never cease to urge his claim, as one of the purest

---

* *Paradiso*, c. iii.

brilliants of his crown. The priest who alarmed the Gallican clergy of 1830 by his ultramontane sympathies with M. de la Mennais, has lived long enough to have a right to protest against the extravagances of some ultramontanes of to-day, and I find in one of his letters, written in the very heat of the enthusiasm inspired by Pius IX., with which he was penetrated as deeply as any, these significant words :

" The papal *omnipotence* is doubtless an ex-
" pression conformable to the doctrine of the
" council of Florence, but one which we must avoid
" using, since the word omnipotence is taken by
" the crowd to mean absolute and arbitrary power,
" whilst nothing is less absolute nor less arbitrary
" than the pontifical power. I have repeated
" opportunities of seeing how extremely important
" it is not to give rise to false ideas upon so
" weighty a point. The old gallicanism is worn
" out, and has scarcely a breath left in it ; but
" the instinctive gallicanism, which consists in
" dreading a power represented as unbounded and
" affecting two hundred millions of individuals
" in every corner of the globe, is a very vital

" and very formidable gallicanism, because founded
" upon a natural and even Christian instinct."

I owe him too this homage, as rarely deserved
as desirable in our times, that in his contro-
versies with the adversaries, not only of his
personal opinions, but of Catholic doctrine, he
ever observed the laws of moderation, urbanity,
and of that respect which fallen and fallible creatures owe each other and their mutual weaknesses.

" I desire," he wrote to me at the outset of
his monastic life, " to become daily more gentle
" towards all, but also more solidly convinced,
" like a blade that becomes flexible in proportion
" to its temper."* He kept his word, and has
thus deserved the beautiful eulogium passed by
him upon Ozanam, who " was gentle to all, and
" just towards error." Yes, *just towards error,*
which is one of the strictest duties of Christian
justice, and one most rigorously incumbent upon
those who have themselves in any way gone
astray.

---

* Nancy, 26th May, 1847.

The great soul of Lacordaire, during his forty years' struggle with the adversaries of Catholicism, was never shut to that compassion which the remembrance of his own short but painful wanderings awoke in him.

He held personal attacks in horror, as well as merciless and insulting zeal, denunciations and imprecations, especially from neophytes. I never saw him more revolted than by the ardour of those converts* " who, in seeking the expression " of their thoughts, never utter anything but an " insult." And, he added, " The convert that *hath* " *not pity* is, in my eyes, a vile creature ; he is " like the centurion on Calvary, who, whilst re- " cognizing Jesus Christ, turned executioner, " instead of striking his breast."†

---

* The word " convert " is here used in the sense not of a man who changes his religion, but who returns to it from infidelity.—[*Translator's Note.*]

† Chalais, September 14th, 1853.

CHAPTER VIII.

HIS POLITICAL ATTITUDE.—THE REVOLUTION OF FEB-
RUARY.—THE ITALIAN AND ROMAN QUESTIONS.

BUT can we say, that, in his political life,
during the short time he mixed in politics, Lacordaire always displayed that sure and sound
judgment which I honor in him? I do not
think so, and I will say why, with the modest
sincerity of a man who has more than once been
himself mistaken, but with the certainty, however,
of finding, in this very criticism, a natural opportunity of defending the memory of a friend from
the unjust and exaggerated attacks of which he
has been the object.

Besides, who can for a moment dream, in this shifting and confused age, of making a crime of a mistake, political or otherwise ? Who is the man so blameless as to be able to throw the first stone ? Error is natural to man ; and I will add, that the motives of error are what determines its moral gravity. When a political mistake, a change of opinion, has been dictated by no selfish fear, no base jealousy, no sordid interest, a man has no reason to blush at it.

Need I say, that the shadow even of such a suspicion cannot rest upon the great and holy memory of Lacordaire.

Let us first of all state that, in politics as in everything else, in spite of contrary appearances, he was always moderate, equally distant from the two extremes. He always energetically scouted the notion of binding himself to any party what-soever. He had in fact no taste for political struggles, and he only found himself engaged in them involuntarily and insensibly, by reason of the great share the question of religious liberty will ever have in these contests. Passionately devoted to liberty, as was for a certain time the whole of his generation, he remained stubbornly true to her.

Born a democrat, he had no difficulty in believing, like all the clear-headed men of this age, in the inevitable triumph of democracy; but he espoused neither its extreme tendencies, nor its bad quarrels. Like the majority of real liberals, he was tolerably indifferent to dynastic questions, and in a certain measure, to forms of government. He always, however, leant towards limited monarchy.*

With regard to the *ensemble* of his judgments touching the state of modern society, I find in one of his old letters, of 1838, an opinion which he constantly professed, which, it seems to me, every enlightened Christian can admit, and which is still, after the two fresh revolutions effected since that date, as sound and judicious as before. " What do we appreciate in the modern times

---

* See especially the *Lettre sur le Saint Siège*, of 1838, which is not contradicted, at least upon the latter point, by his last publication of 1860, on the Italian question.

" which began with the American Revolution in
" 1776 ? We appreciate in them the ruin of three
" elements subversive of the Catholic Church, our
" eternal country; absolutism, gallicanism, and
" rationalism.

" We love the present time because it is
" sapping the absolute power of princes, and
" raising the human mind, ground down for the
" last three centuries under brute force.

" Without approving any specific act of re-
" volutions we assist at them as at a great divine
" retribution, a great drama in which is being
" played out the liberation of the Church, and in
" her the liberation of humanity. But this drama
" is confused in its details, made up of good and
" evil ; it is one in which Robespierre appears by
" the side of Washington, M. Isambert* beside
" M. de Merode,† and where conscience at every

---

* A deputy famous, under the reign of Louis Philippe, by
his bigoted attacks upon the clergy.—[*Translator's Note.*]

† A Catholic nobleman, whose patriotism and high position
placed him at the head of the Provisional Government of

" moment stumbles in its appreciation of a thou-
" sand different elements. It is a picture of
" chaos breathed upon by the Holy Ghost; the
" *fiat lux* has not yet been heard. Again, we love
" the present time because it is grinding to dust
" the frightful spirit of gallicanism, that slow
" and treacherous schism which divides whilst
" appearing to unite, which leaves the devil at his
" ease, and conscience contented.

"Lastly, we love those terrible blows dealt
" out to rationalism by its powerlessness to build
" up anything whatever. . . . . We love then
" the present inasmuch as it is ruining the past,
" and appears to tend towards a future for Catho-
" licism, big with the liberation of the Church
" and the world, but we cannot accept the re-
" sponsibility of its acts. A politician, by the
" nature of his functions, can and must accept this
" responsibility ; a religious, a man of the future,
" has to remain like Moses upon the mountain,—

_____

Belgium, after the revolution of September 1880.—[*Translator's Note.*]

" to lift up his hands for Israel, to speak the truth
" to that half-free, half-enslaved people, which one
" day adores the golden calf, and the next prays
" at the entrance of the tabernacle."*

These last words remind me that the momentary severity of his judgment upon contemporary France did not shut out from his heart a tender and ardent patriotism. †

" A country has been seen," he said, at the beginning of his polemical struggles, " which is
" neither enslaved nor free, the wretched play-
" thing of two contrary ideas, the love of liberty and
" distrust of God, and yet the noblest country on
" earth, and the happiest, as soon as it shall have

---

* Metz, 14th March, 1838.

† " France is what she is, and not what you imagine her
" to be; she is a country which has never once in three
" centuries understood the meaning of liberty, a country in
" which some are afraid of Mass, and all of inequality of
" rank, and in which these two ideas make up the sum total
" of current philosophy."—La Chesnaie, 2nd November, 1832.

" In France it is not freedom, but religion, which is want-
" ing; it is not the king, but the people, who is unworthy."—
15th March, 1833.

" united in its love what its chiefs have severed " in their politics : our beloved land, France !"*

Who can help admiring, nay, envying the touching confidence, the filial tenderness which dictated the dedication of that *Memorial in favor of the re-establishment of the Friars-Preachers in France*, in which he seems to stand forward as one of those supplicant exiles of antiquity, who used to come and ask for an asylum by clasping the domestic altars of their hosts ?

" My Country,

" Whilst thou art pursuing in joy and pain " the formation of modern society, one of thy " youngest children, by faith a Christian, a priest " by the traditional unction of the Church, comes " and asks thee for his share of the liberties thou " hast won. He begs thee to read the memorial he " presents to thee, so that, knowing his desires, his " rights, his very heart, thou mayest afford him " that protection which thou wilt ever extend to

---

* Extracts from the *Avenir*, vol. i., p. 423. Article on the obsequies of Gregory XVI.

" what is useful and sincere. Mayest thou, my
" country, never despair of thy cause,—vanquish
" ill-fortune by patience, and good-fortune by jus-
" tice towards thy enemies ; love God, who is the
" Father of all thou lovest ; prostrate thyself be-
" fore his Son Jesus Christ, the liberator of the
" world ; yield to no one the eminent post thou
" fillest in creation, and find better but not more
" devoted servants than myself !"

And this conclusion of the same document :

" Whatever the treatment reserved for me by
" my country, I shall not then complain ; I will
" hope in her until my last breath. I understand
" her very injustices, I respect her very errors :
" not like the courtier who adores his master,
" but like the friend who knows by what links
" evil is connected with good in the depths of
" his friend's heart. These sentiments are too
" deeply rooted in me ever to die, and should
" I not be destined to reap the fruit of them,
" they will remain to the last my guests and my
" consolation."

How then, seeing this exquisite sentiment of
dignity and moderation, to which I am not tired

of calling attention, did he allow himself, once or twice in his life, to be prevailed upon to take up a position which confounded and afflicted his oldest and most tried friends ? I can account for it by nothing but the only weakness I ever re- marked in him, namely, a too great indulgence to- wards those immoral and essentially revolutionary politics, the formula of which is well known, "*He who wills the end, wills the means.*" He cer- tainly did not, like some of our modern reformers, profess the sovereignty of the end*; but when this end appeared to him lawful, glorious, necessary, and popular, he was too much inclined to excuse the injustice and violence which had effected it.

And yet, what more uncertain here below, what more deceitful, than the object of our la- bours, our undertakings, our very sacrifices ? The Christian knows but one only infallible and neces- sary end,—the salvation of his soul. In every-

---

* *La souveraineté du but.* It was thus that Barbes, one of the revolutionary chiefs in 1848, defined the object of their policy.

thing else the honor and merit of life consist simply in the choice and use of the means.

" It does not suffice," said Bossuet, " for the " good man to will only what is just ; he fears to " tarnish the purity of his innocent designs, he " wills only good means to effect them, and he is " ever mindful of that precept of the law, ' Thou " ' shalt pursue justly that which is just'—' *Juste* " *quod justum est persequeris.*' "*

The end may be trivial, it may be a mistaken one ; but if it be attained solely by honest means, approved of by conscience, the agent is blameless.

On the contrary, he may aspire to an end really or apparently very useful and very lofty ; but if he attain it by criminal or ignoble means, his success is vain, he merits neither honour, esteem, nor sympathy. This elementary doctrine of public and private morality seems to me to have been occasionally lost sight of by Lacordaire in his purely political appreciations.

---

* *On Ambition*, Fragment iii., 146, edition of Versailles.

He so pure, so generous, so incapable of re-volutionary baseness, forgave and forgot it too easily in the champions of his chosen cause.

Those triumphs of violence which favoured his opinions, without procuring him any personal advantage, did not inspire him with that healthy distrust so well expressed by his saintly and witty friend, Madame Swetchine, when she said : " I " have never dreaded but one thing, and that is " the absolute triumph of any one." Thus it is that we may account for his assent to the Revo-lution of February, and the Italian Revolution.

I carefully distinguish between the Revolution of February and the Republic. In the republican form there was nothing of a nature to wound Lacordaire or force him to inaction. He had condemned it beforehand, in one of his previous productions, with a severity which was even then bitterly reproached to him,* and which had

---

* " We may discover in the lowest class of society a certain " faction which imagines itself to be republican, of which it " would not be worth while to speak, if it had not a chance

burst forth still more freely in his letters, and his private conversations : " If we get a republic, it " would make us either die of laughter or of " fright." *

But this prediction was intended less for the Republic itself than for the Republicans, such as he had known them in his youth, as may be seen from the following still more prophetic passage :

" If the Republicans, that is the ambitious " dregs of every town and village, get the upper " hand, they will be the horror of liberty . . . . . . " and France exhausted, will throw herself into " the arms of a master, who will do whatever he " pleases with us."† In the main the Republic, taken apart from its authors and creatures, differs too slightly from royalty as laid down in the Charta, to prevent its being accepted honorably by the partisans of the latter. As we have just

---

" of cutting off our heads in the interim between two mon-
" archies."—*Lettre sur le Saint Siège*, 1838.
    * 11th December, 1832.
    † La Chesnaie, 2nd November, 1832.

been reminded by a great authority, between a constitutional monarchy and a republic the difference is superficial; whilst between a constitutional and an absolute monarchy the difference is fundamental.*

Consequently Lacordaire could, without inconsistency, hail the advent of the Republic with confidence and joy. He associated himself with that group of fervent Catholics who believed that 1848 was the dawn of a *New Era*. They gave their paper this name, preached in it the acceptance of the new state of things, and proclaimed the necessary connection between Christianity and democracy with an honest but intemperate zeal, which was not shared in,† but could not sufficiently be got under by him who had so eloquently combatted the doctrine of the necessary connection between Catholicism and monarchy.

---

* Benjamin Constant, quoted by M. Edward la Boulaye in his fine essay in the *Revue Nationale*.

† " This paper goes far beyond my ideas in democracy, " and all its editors well know how I have struggled to get it " to adopt a more reserved line."—Chalais, 7th November, 1848.

He was returned to the Constituent Assembly; and no one can reproach him for having taken his seat in an assembly, which counted among its members three bishops and twenty priests.

All who remember those days will agree with me that his election reassured and delighted all religious men.   He had not come forward of his own accord as candidate; his place was thrust upon him, both by the fervent wishes of Catholics and the sympathies of the people, which his resolute and independent attitude under the former government had gained for him.

These sympathies manifested themselves in the acclamations with which the crowd greeted him when he appeared with the Assembly upon the steps of the Palais-Bourbon, to proclaim the Republic.   His legislative campaign, however, was not a long one.   It lasted ten days.   During this short space of time he twice addressed the House, but with no success.

I saw him sitting in his place, impassible, on the invasion of the 15th of May, marked out above all, by his white habit, to the threats of the rioters.

The next day he handed in his resignation ; he saw, with the prudence I have already praised in him, that his character, both impetuous and meditative, was not adapted to the sudden every-day storms of parliamentary life.

On the 26th of May, he announced his intention of retiring from the editorship of the *Ere Nouvelle*, in a letter which I have in my possession. At the request of his collaborators he consented to defer the execution of his resolution until September 1848, when he finally retired from that paper.

Even before this final separation he had sought quiet in the convent of his order, founded by him in the rural solitude of Chalais, not far from the Grande-Chartreuse, the memory of which inspired him with one of the most beautiful pages of the *Memoirs,* dedicated by him on his death-bed, and looked for by the public with such reasonable impatience.

His retirement did not prevent him from following, with attentive solicitude, all discussions touching religious liberty, and especially that concerning the law, presented by M. de Falloux, to ensure Freedom of Education. Unlike those writers whom the clergy have adopted as their oracles, he cordially hailed this law, and, however modified it may have become by subsequent legislation, he compared it lately, very happily and rightly, to the Edict of Nantes, "that great act which, for a " century, was the honor of France, and the fruit-" ful principle of the intellectual and moral eleva-" tion of her Church."

With what then can he be reproached during this critical phase of his life ? Certainly not, once more, with having accepted the Republic and a seat in the legislature ; but with having approved the Revolution of February, and, on his first appearance in the tribune, with having, after M. de Lamartine, sided with those who were most deeply compromised in it : with not having discerned the odious injustice and unpardonable futility of this revolution, in which a giddy people shattered, like a toy, a legality which the government had scrupulously respected, and a constitution which either contained or admitted of every liberty and every progress : with having chosen for the starting point of an era of salvation and reparation that lamentable catastrophe which has everywhere thrown back either liberty or justice; that mad step, forced upon a great nation, which only escaped the most cruel trials by an unlooked-for favor of Providence, when it fell into the hands of a group of men still more astonished than pleased at their triumph, and far more honorable and moderate than their army : men whose moderation and integrity have honored their ephemeral omnipotence.

This much said, let us do Lacordaire the justice to state that, even in the midst of this illusion, he ever maintained the dignity which was natural to him. He hailed the victors with simple courtesy, nothing more ; he spared the vanquished all recrimination and insult ; he never knew that cowardly ferocity towards the defeated which among us but too frequently dishonors the victorious party. He was true to his natural magnanimity, when, appearing, three days after the fall of the throne, in the pulpit of Notre Dame to commence his seventh station, he addressed these words to the Archbishop, whose appointment he had so eagerly desired, and whose

glorious death was soon to warrant and surpass
our expectations :

"My Lord,—The Church and the country
"thank you for the example you have given us
"all in these days of great and memorable emo-
"tion. You have summoned us to this Cathedral
"on the morrow of a revolution, in which every-
"thing seemed lost. We have come ; we are here,
"tranquil, beneath these aged vaults ; we learn
"from them to fear nothing for religion and
"France ; both are advancing under the hand
"of God who shields them ; both thank you for
"having believed in their indissoluble alliance,
"and for having distinguished from the things
"that pass, those which gain strength from the
"very uncertainty of events."

Equity, too, obliges us to hear him himself
explaining, in the calm of retirement, after the
lapse of many years, his thoughts and desires
at that period. "I did not, even then, agree
"with Ozanam's views. I did not want to dis-
"cuss theoretically the question of democracy,
"but to confine myself to the acceptance of a
"fact, and to turn it to the best account for the

" good of religion and society. . . . . I ac-
" cepted the Republic which gave us liberty of in-
" struction, and the freedom of religious bodies, and
" which was only destroyed by violence, thanks
" to the impatience and clumsiness of the royalists.
" Even from my point of view, I can very well
" conceive how people could accept the Republic
" simply for a time ; but they ought to have
" behaved themselves so as not to get something
" worse, and to throw France into the moral pros-
" tration in which we see her. The Republic
" was a means and a lesson ; they ought to have
" understood it, supported it, looked to the future,
" repelled, instead of inviting pretenders, and not
" ruined everything by over haste."*

Without being very warm royalists we might
have answered, " The Republic, too, was the
" offspring of violence, of unprovoked violence ;
" it only perished because the Republicans turned
" the head of France by the panic created by

---

* Sorèze. September 8th, 1855.

" their doctrines of spoliation, their apologies of
" a bloody past, and their tumultuous rudeness
" in both Assemblies." Barnave had foretold its
fate, as well as that of its predecessor, when he
said, " There are two things, without which gene-
" rous and civilized nations cannot do : peace and
" liberty. But, for the ordinary run of men,
" peace is more necessary than liberty. Liberty
" is a superfluity which creates happiness : unless
" you ally both, you render both impossible ;
" if you give the nation riotous liberty, beware,
" lest you see the majority destroy liberty rather
" than condemn itself to a perpetual state of agi-
" tation and suspense."*

I trust I shall be excused for dwelling a little
longer, perhaps too long, upon this stormy epoch,
in order to recount an incident calculated to display the innate nobleness of Lacordaire's character, and his inviolable fidelity to friendship.

---

* Speech of August 31st, 1791.

It was on the 11th of April, 1848. Lacordaire had been invited to put forth his political and religious opinions in presence of the Club *de l' Union*, held in the great hall of the Sorbonne, whither flocked two or three thousand hearers, whilst an immense crowd, unable to get into the body of the building, swarmed into the court, and disturbed, by its songs and cries, the interrogatories and discussions within.

A person, styling himself Citizen Barnabé Chauvelot, took it into his head to question him concerning his relations with me. Precisely at that time we were more divided than ever before or since. He had neither shared the apprehension, nor approved the forebodings I experienced at the violence of the liberal party in Belgium, the impious oppression of the little Swiss cantons, the crushing of the Sonderbund by mere numerical strength, and the growing audacity of the radicals. Since the proclamation of the Republic, we had scarcely seen each other.

His natural generosity, however, immediately overcame the fear of wounding that fiery audience.

Calm and intrepid in the midst of the tumult, he took up my defence. I copy the reporter's return of that sitting.*

" *Citizen Barnabé.*—I ask Citizen Lacordaire " whether he shares the opinions put forth by the " Citizen Montalembert, in a speech made in the " House of Peers, upon the Swiss question ? . . . ."

" *Citizen Lacordaire.*— . . . . Citizens, you " have put the following question to me : ' Do you " ' approve of the speech of M. de Montalembert ?' " I distinguish : In my opinion M. de Montalem-" bert has not thoroughly mastered the question. " He has only looked at the danger incurred by " religious liberty ; the question of Helvetian " unity and nationality were also to be examined. " For my own part, if I had had to discuss " this question, I should have established that " Switzerland had a right to will Helvetian unity,

---

* *Biographie des Candidats à l'Assemblée Nationale, par un Vieux Montagnard.* Lacordaire (Henri) devant le Club de l'Union. Stenographié par Corby (Alfred), Paris, Librairie républicaine de Gustave Havard, 24, Rue des Mathurins S. Jacques. 1848. 24mo. 52 pages.

" and that, consequently, all the movements going
" forward in that country, ought not to be con-
" founded with anti-religious movements. I think,
" then, that M. de Montalembert has seen only a
" part, and not the whole of the question. But
" whenever an orator has views, which, although
" perhaps not complete, are prompted by a firm
" heart, inclined to liberty, the liberty of all
" nations; I think it is a duty to show oneself
" more than indulgent to that man. I should not
" have said what he has said, but still his speech
" does not prevent me from recognizing in M. de
" Montalembert a good Frenchman, a man of
" talent, devoted to the commonwealth; and con-
" sequently I have remained penetrated with
" esteem and friendship for him.

" *The Citizen Barnabé.*—The question put by
" me to the candidate was not a religious question;
" I simply asked Father Lacordaire whether he
" adopted the judgment passed by the Citizen
" Montalembert, upon liberals in general, and
" upon the men of '93 in particular.

" *The Citizen Lacordaire.*—The Citizen Mon-
" talembert, in his speech, has passed a judgment

" upon what he calls the past and present radicals,
" the radicals of 1793 and the radicals of 1847.
" For my part I declare that I am not in the
" slightest degree radical, in the sense usually
" given to that word.

" The word radical, too, bears a meaning in
" our language, which up to the present is not
" favorable . . . . . (The candidate is interrupted.
" Division in the hall . . . . Clamour out-
" side.)

" Gentlemen, in one word, M. de Montalembert
" has spoken somewhat ill of 1793. Well, for
" my part, I declare there are some of the men
" of '93 of whom I could never speak well ; that
" there were in 1847, in 1848, and that there
" will be in 1849, speeches and acts of certain
" revolutionists of which I never could speak well.
" Now who are these revolutionists ? They are
" those who don't want liberty in order, and order
" in liberty. I look upon order and liberty as
" two essential elements of human life, and who-
" ever is convicted of having been the enemy of
" order, he is the enemy of liberty. (Fresh clamour
" outside.—Silence restored after some time.) I

" despise tyrants because they are the enemies
" of liberty; I despise the revolutionists, because,
" bearing another name, they were at bottom
" tyrants.　Between tyrants and these revolu-
" tionists I make no distinction.

" *The Citizen Barnabé.*—The answer does not
" appear to me categorical.　I ask Citizen Lacor-
" daire whether that speech, which was a long
" venomous satire upon our fathers of '93, de-
" serves praise or blame ?

" *Citizen Lacordaire.*—I am told *categorically*
" that the speech of Citizen Montalembert was
" against our fathers of '93.　Well, for my part
" I declare I recognize no father of '93.　I
" recognize in 1789 a large number of men who
" wanted the destruction of abuses, and who
" struggled for that destruction.　I recognize from
" '89 to '93 men who died combatting these
" abuses, both in the interior on the scaffold, and
" out of the country in the battle-field.　Men who
" hold to their purpose, in the struggle for liberty,
" such men I call my fathers.　Among those who
" died at this time, I distinguish those who died
" to defend this liberty, and those who put others

" to death in order to stifle and annihilate this " liberty."

I imagine that such language, spoken in the National Assembly, would have gone far enough to secure him a place in it, but the retirement which enabled him again to mount the pulpit of Notre Dame was undoubtedly better for him. What adds to the generosity displayed in this stormy incident is, that he never uttered a word about it to him whom he had thus defended ; and it was only long afterwards that I came to know it, by the discovery of the obscure pamphlet from which these details are taken. I was the more touched at this, inasmuch as I had met with not only certain Republicans of the eve, but also some Catholics, who assured me my career was at an end, according to the axiom so current in France : " You have protested against those " who have become the masters ; you are now " powerless for yourself and for us."

The same illusion which I pointed out above caused him to assume, with regard to the Italian question, an attitude which surprised and afflicted the majority of his friends and admirers.

It did him all the more harm inasmuch as it was shared in by many less Catholics than his assent to the Revolution of February.

He did not early enough distinguish the evident dangers inseparable from the line followed by the Italian patriots. The sacred and lawful end aimed at by them in emancipating Italy from a foreign yoke, concealed from him too long the profound immorality of the means employed. He had too easily forgiven the Italians of 1848, for having so badly served their noble cause, at a moment when everything favored them; for having suffered Rossi to be assassinated, Pius IX. driven out, and Charles Albert to be fired at in the streets of Milan, without having uttered a single serious protest against these atrocious follies. Having given up reading the newspapers, he was but ill acquainted with the vexations, the spoliations, and humiliations which M. de Cavour had heaped upon the Church in Piedmont, from his very accession to power; as though designedly to estrange Catholics from the Italian movement, by giving them just cause for repugnance and regret. Finally, and I say it with pain, he sometimes seemed to lean towards that dangerous sophism, which attempts to excuse persecutors and despoilers, because the Church has always issued triumphant from persecution and spoliation.

He hailed the war of 1859 because he believed it just and favorable to the emancipation of a Christian people, and because he believed in the promises which guaranteed to the Catholic world " the respect of all the rights of the Holy See." But although his opinions, uselessly divulgated at that time, have often been quoted as an argument against ours, we must acknowledge that he never pushed enthusiasm and confidence as far as some bishops, as for instance, Monseigneur de Salinis, archbishop of Auch, who said to his clergy, " It is not the Revolution, it is our own " France which has crossed the Alps after the " Emperor : the France of Charlemagne and St. " Louis."*

At the conclusion of the war, when the greed

---

* Circular to the clergy of the diocese of Auch, May 1859.

of Piedmont showed itself in all its nudity, when the perils and trials of the Holy Father began to thicken, the priest and the Catholic again displayed themselves to the full in Lacordaire.

The *unification* of Italy, that fatal utopy, invented by revolutionary despotism to estrange for ever from the Italian cause Catholic hearts, inspired him with neither confidence nor sympathy. His correspondents in Italy know well with what energy he reproached M. de Cavour and his " anti-social and anti-Christian policy " with having forced the Holy See to spurn the idea of an arrangement ; and how, from the date of the invasion of the Roman and Neapolitan states, he acknowledged that the Italian Revolution had fallen a prey to the spirit " of usurpation " and conquest."

As early as the 27th of January, 1860, he wrote to M. Cochin :

" I am obliged to you for having put an end to " the abuse made of two imperfectly known letters " written at the beginning of the Italian war, " whilst as yet nothing had happened to damp " my wishes and my hopes : they could have no

" bearing upon a state of things the novelty of
" which is but too evident and too regrettable.
" Pius IX. is now too much like Pius VII. in his
" misfortunes, as he has been in his generous
" plans, to permit anything but filial piety to
" rule my thoughts and words."

The ingratitude of the Italians towards Pius
IX. had long shocked him. " This is the really
" strong point of the defence of that generous
" and unfortunate pontiff. Posterity may perhaps
" lay a little to his charge, but his virtue, his
" goodness, his magnanimous designs, will turn
" the scale of the future, and plead, together with
" his cause, that of the papacy."*

"One day," he said later on, "when the
" stranger shall no longer reign in Italy, when
" her own mistress, rescued from irreligion by
" liberty, she shall look back upon the time when
" she was struggling upwards towards her destiny,
" the image of an unfortunate pontiff will rise

---

* 10th September, 1856.

" before her pacified eyes ; she will recognize in
" his sad and calm features the greatest hero of
" her independence, the man who would have
" spared her cause blood, tears, shame, and re-
" morse ; and, too slow in justice, if ever it is
" too late to be just, she will raise a statue to
" the Washington that God gave her, and whom
" she refused." *

It is true, that, being an intrepid champion and
devoted child of the papacy ; that having given
constant and memorable proofs of his devotedness,
he considered himself entitled to desire for the
Roman States a system of administration other
than the one of which he summed up the danger,
weakness, and defence by qualifying it as a
government of the old régime. In 1838, in that
magnificent apology of the papacy, in which he
represents the Holy See as " ever insulted in the
" interim between her past and future glory, like
" Jesus Christ crucified in time, between the day

-----

* *De la Liberté de l'Eglise et de l'Italie,* p. 35.

"of creation and that of eternal judgment," he had done his best to dispel the error which identified the cause of Rome with that of absolute governments, and made her out to be the enemy of all countries whose institutions recalled the ancient liberties of Catholic Europe.*

Ever faithful to the memory of the enthusiasm created by the first years of the pontificate of Pius IX., he believed neither in the utility nor the possibility of that eternal *status quo*, the results of which have been so disastrous.

" Yes," he said, " the head of universal Chris-
" tendom, the highest organ of that Gospel which
" has saved the human race ; yes, that man must
" be a sovereign ; but he must be an able sove-
" reign ; one who administers his states well, and
" knows how to acquire in them the moral power
" which may uphold him." †

He would undoubtedly never have been one of those who reproached the papacy with its

---

* *Lettre sur le Saint Siège.* Preface to 1st edition.
† 9th August, 1856.

immobility, because it upholds the eternal laws of justice, by refusing to ratify, even implicitly, spoliation. But he acknowledged the right of no abuse to legalize itself by age.

He was ever hoping to see the pontiff enter spontaneously, and of his own authority, into the way of reforms, and thus form in Italy an honest and enlightened Christian party.

" I am for the Holy See against its oppressors; " I believe in the moral necessity of its temporal " power, I compassionate with it in its misfortunes, " I would willingly give the last drop of my " blood for it; but, at the same time, I desire the " freedom of Italy, serious changes in the govern- " ment of the Roman States, and a still more " important change in that moral direction of " which, in these latter times, the *Univers* and " the *Civiltà Cattolica* are the summary."*

But not more than the learned and conscientious Döllinger, whose wishes so frequently

---

* 11th February, 1860.

squared with his own, did he consent to the least suppression or diminution of that pontifical power, to whose regeneration he looked forward.

His last publication, *De la Liberté de l'Italie et de l'Eglise*, which appeared almost immediately after his election to the Academy, has put an end to whatever doubts might have existed on this point.* Eloquent like all that he ever wrote, but calm, equitable, impartial, at once *"free and "respectful,"* this protest had the double advantage of silencing those who accused the illustrious religious of want of filial piety towards Rome, and of preventing his pure and glorious name from being for the future quoted by the partisans of Piedmont, by the admirers of the d'Azeglios, and the Passaglias.

From that moment, those who set up the Italian sympathies of Lacordaire against the unanimous indignation of the Catholic world, could no longer class him amongst their authorities.

---

* February 1860.

He was not the man to blaspheme Rome in her misfortunes, and commit the crime of Cham, —that crime which has " been visited on earth " by the most palpable and lasting of chastise- " ments."

He was not the man to sacrifice the principle of the pontifical royalty, he who, twenty years before, when speaking in the pulpit of Notre-Dame on the vocation of the French nation, had thus spoken of the creation of that royalty : " At a time when the papacy, but just snatched " from the treacherous hands of the lower em- " pire, was threatened with the yoke of a bar- " barous power, France secured its liberty and " dignity, first by arms, and then definitely by " a territorial grant, to which was annexed sove- " reignty. The head of the Church, thanks to " Charlemagne, ceased to be dependent upon an " authority which had, by the formation of " modern nations, more than ever lost its cha- " racter of universality ; and he was able to stretch " out over the natioאs, whose common father he " was, a peace-bearing sceptre. . . . . " This great work was ours ; I say ours, for are

R

" not our fathers ourselves ?   Do we not live in
" them, and they in us ?   Did they not desire
" that we should be what they were, a generation
" of knights-defenders of the Church ? *

" We may then say, confounding father and
" son with lawful pride . . . . we vanquished
" Arius, Mahomet, Luther, and founded the tem-
" poral power of the popes.   Arianism defeated,
" Mahometanism defeated, Protestantism defeated,
" *a throne secured for the pontificate ;* such are
" the four crowns of France, crowns that will not
" fade in eternity."†

Are they not the same accents which, twenty
years later, on the verge of the tomb, burst forth
in these cruelly true words : " Italians, your cause
" is grand ; but you do not know how to honor

---

* This is literally verified in the illustrious author of this
memoir.   The name of his ancestors figures in the list of the
noble crusaders, who, in the *dark* ages, went forth against
Islam.—[*Translator's Note.*]

† Sermon preached at Notre-Dame on the 14th of February, 1841, on occasion of the inauguration of the Friars-
Preachers in France.

" it.   Rome wanted nothing but time and the
" help of your reconquered liberties. . . . .
" For a vain system of numerical and absolute
" unity, which has no bearing upon your nation-
" ality and liberty, you have raised between you
" and two hundred millions of Catholics a barrier
" which is daily increasing in height.   You have
" enlisted against your most lawful cause more
" than men ; you have enlisted against it Chris-
" tianity :   that is to say, God's greatest work
" upon earth, his visible light and goodness, the
" empire of souls, the rock upon which all hostile
" designs have split. . . . .   You have enlisted
" against you an eternal decree of God.   One
" day, without doubt, you will stumble on that
" rock." *

The following letter addressed by Lacordaire,
nineteen days before his death, to M. Guizot,
touching the generous plea put forth by that
eminent statesman in favor of the pontifical cause,

---

* *De la Liberté de l'Italie et de l'Eglise*, p. 36.

will not be without its interest. It is, I think, the last letter he was able to dictate before his agony. Posterity will not disdain this interchange of sympathies upon the greatest and most imperilled interest of our times, between the Catholic religious and the Protestant statesman, both illustrious among the illustrious, and both superior to the violence as well as to the injustice of party-spirit:

"Sorèze, November 2nd, 1861.

"Sir and dear Colleague,*

"I had just finished reading your work "upon the 'Church and Christian Society in "1861,' when I received a second copy, sent to "me by your orders, together with your note of "October 29th. This mark of your remembrance "was the more agreeable to me as I was still "under the pleasurable impression which your "book had made upon me. It is a great light "coming from a great authority.

----

* It will be remembered that both were Academicians.

" You will readily understand that I cannot
" agree with you upon the theological question of
" Protestantism ; I would also make a reserva-
" tion upon the Italian question up to the time
" when Piedmont invaded the Neapolitan States,
" and a portion of the States of the Church,
" which had been kept in regular obedience to
" the pope. It was at this point, so it seems
" to me, that justification ceased to be possible,
" and that the Italian Revolution assumed a cha-
" racter of violence, conquest, and usurpation.

" With regard to the broad views of your
" work,—the errors and merits of our times,—to
" what is wanting to us in prosperity and ad-
" versity,—to the necessity of serious religious
" liberty for the good of the state and of all
" Christian communities,—to the difference be-
" tween the *liberal* and *revolutionary* spirit,—to
" our fears and hopes for the future, I look upon
" your ideas as the only ones calculated to save
" the world and the Church.

" You must necessarily, sir and honored col-
" league, have suffered many attacks ; but you
" are long used to them, and it is impossible to

" serve men without exposing oneself to their
" ingratitude.

" My health, after which you do me the honor
" to ask, is still very uncertain, and makes me
" envy your green old age, which has nowise suf-
" fered from such great and protracted labors.

" I have the honor to be, &c.,

" BR. HENRY DOMINIC LACORDAIRE,
" *Of the Friars-Preachers.*"

(Signed with his hand.)

CHAPTER IX.

HIS LAST CONFERENCES.—HIS OPINION UPON THE NEW
ATTITUDE OF THE CLERGY.—HIS RETIREMENT AT
SORÈZE.—HIS DEATH.

WE must now conclude ; the more so because we
do not enjoy the liberty necessary to speak upon
the last ten years of his life, with the fulness and
sincerity which has hitherto presided at our work.
Let us then remind our readers that Lacordaire,
delivered of his seat in the Constituent Assembly,
again ascended the pulpit of Notre-Dame, and
occupied it during the three years 1849, 1850,
and 1851. These three stations were devoted to

the " *Commerce of Man with God, the Fall and*
" *Reinstatement of Man, and the Providential*
" *Economy of the Reparation.*" In April 1851,
no alarming symptom gave reason to fear that
this pulpit, so long and nobly filled by him, was
about to be closed to him ; and yet, as though
by a secret foreboding, which he disallowed even
whilst giving vent to it, he felt himself impelled to
close the station by a solemn farewell, which
ought to be given here, because it contains a kind
of summary of his previous life, and is one of
the very rare occasions on which the orator re-
verted to himself personally :

" Even although a continuance of my labors
" among you were prepared for me by God and
" my love for you, I cannot prevent myself from
" speaking as though I were bidding you farewell.
" Allow me to do so, not as a foreboding of the
" future, but as a consolation.

" I say a consolation, because I am a prey to
" two different feelings, one of joy at having com-
" pleted with you a task favorable to the salva-
" tion of many, and at having completed it in an
" age called the age of abortions ; the other of

" sadness, at thinking that man completes nothing
" without spending upon it the better portion
" of himself, the prime of his strength and the
" flower of his years. Dante thus begins his
" divine song : ' In the middle of the path of life,
" ' I awoke alone in a dense forest.' I have come,
" gentlemen, to that middle point of the path of
" life, in which man is stripped of the last ray of
" his youth, and rapidly sinks down to the region
" of powerlessness and oblivion. I ask nothing
" better than to sink down to it, since it is the
" just portion assigned us by Providence ; but at
" least at this boundary, from whence I can once
" more contemplate the times that are about to
" end, you will not envy me the happiness of
" casting back a glance, and of awaking before
" you, the companions of my journey, some of
" the memories which render so dear to me both
" this cathedral and yourselves.

" Here it was that, when my soul had re-
" covered the light of God, I received forgiveness
" of my faults, and I see the altar where upon my
" lips, strengthened by age, and purified by re-
" pentance, I received for the second time the

" God who had visited me at the first dawn of
" my youth.

" Here it was that, prostrate upon the pave-
" ment of the temple, I mounted by degrees to
" the priesthood, and where, after I had long
" sought for the secret of my vocation, it was
" revealed to me in this pulpit, which for the last
" seventeen years you have surrounded with
" silence and honor. It was here that, returning
" from a voluntary exile, I brought back the
" religious habit which half a century of pro-
" scription had banished from Paris, and that,
" presenting it to an assembly formidable by its
" number and diversity, it won your unanimous
" respect.

" Here it was that on the morrow of a revo-
" lution, when our places were still covered with
" the ruins of the throne and the symbols of war,
" you came to listen to the word which outlives
" every ruin, and which, backed by an irre-
" sistible emotion, you that day hailed with
" applause.

" It is here, under the stones near the altar,
" that sleep my two first archbishops : he who

" called me, still young, to the honor of instruct-
" ing you ;* and he who recalled me after distrust
" of my own strength had separated us.† It is
" here, upon this same archiepiscopal seat, that I
" have found, in a third pontiff,‡ the same love
" and the same protection.

" In short, it is here that were begot all the
" affections which have been the consolation of
" my life, and that a lone man, unknown to
" the great, a stranger to parties, and to those
" resorts where crowds meet and friendships are
" formed, I found the souls that have loved me.

" O, sacred walls of Notre-Dame, sacred vaults
" that have carried my words to so many intellects
" deprived of God, altars which have blessed me,
" I do not leave you ; I do but say what you
" have been to a man, and melt within myself
" at the remembrance of your blessings, like the
" children of Israel who, both at home and in
" exile, celebrated the memory of Sion.

" And you, gentlemen, generation already

---

* Mgr. de Quelen.   † Mgr. Affre.   ‡ Mgr. Sibour.

" numerous, in whom perhaps I have implanted
" truths and virtues, I am bound to you for the
" future as I have been during the past; but if
" one day my strength should be unequal to my
" will, if you should come to disdain the re-
" mains of a voice once dear to you, know that
" you will never be ungrateful, for nothing can
" for the future prevent you from having been
" the glory of my life, and from being my crown
" in eternity."

Such was his farewell to the pulpit of Notre-
Dame. After the *coup d'état* of the 2nd of
December, 1851, he never re-ascended it. The
last time he was heard in Paris was at St. Roch,
on the 10th of February, 1853, in that same
church where twenty years before he had stam-
mered out his first sermon.

He came to preach a sermon in presence of
the Archbishop of Paris and Cardinal Donnet, in
favor of the Ecoles Chrétiennes.

He took for his text the words addressed by
David at his death to his son Solomon, "*Esto vir*,"
and his discourse turned upon the obligations of
Christian manliness in public and private life.

Although the next day's *Moniteur* contained a flattering analysis of this sermon, it awoke great susceptibilities, and was looked upon as a hostile demonstration against the new government. This appreciation was a singularly exaggerated one. I have under my eyes several different short-hand copies of this improvisation, which has never been published, and I find in it nothing which surpasses, or even equals, his ordinary boldness. The subject is not exhausted, far from it; it is scarcely more than skimmed over in one or two powerful strokes.

He endeavoured chiefly to show in what consists greatness of character, and how it is a strict and rigorous duty of the Christian.

"The practice of the greatness of the Gospel," he said, "is incompatible with meanness of cha-
" racter. . . . . It is well," he added, "that
" we should know what we mean by making
" Christians ; whether we intend to make real
" men or vulgar men ; whether for us man is
" the *homo*, whom the ancients derived from
" *humus*, earth, slime ; or the *vir*, the man who
" is something more than earth, who has courage,

"soul, virtue, *virtus.* . . . . A man may have
"a great mind and a vulgar soul, an intellect
"capable of enlightening his age, and a soul
"capable of dishonoring it: he may be a great
"man in mind, and a wretch at heart. *He who
"employs vile means even to do good, even to save
"his country, is never anything but a villain.*"*

He then mingled with his religious consider-
ations an eloquent apology of ancient literature,
which certain Catholic writers were already beginning to decry, and which he was fond of
considering as the vestibule of Christianity.

He did not forget his dear Roman senate,
"next to the English parliament, the most illus-
"trious assembly in the world, the latter having
"over it the advantage of being an assembly of
"Christians."

Passing to another order of ideas, he said,

---

* This passage was construed as a demonstration against
the Emperor Napoleon III., whose course it will be remembered excited such deep and bitter indignation in England at
that time. The reader will probably think of the familiar
proverb of the "cap."—[*Translator's Note.*]

" God brings about so many events in order to
" create here and there illustrious misfortune,
" and men who know how to esteem it ; God is
" busied with giving us opportunities of weeping.
" He overthrows empires, He raises up others, not
" for what you may imagine, but in order that
" there may be tears, and that there being tears,
" there may be martyrs, sufferers, men who in
" trial display that grand character which alone
" lends dignity to adversity."

Hence a magnificent development upon the
Revolution, preceded by the conspiracy of the
princes of the earth, and the princes of intellect
to despoil and dishonor the Church. " The Church
" of France voluntarily gave up her wealth when
" asked ; she went into exile when required ; she
" laid her head upon the block when told to do
" so ; and thus, in a few days, she saved the faith
" in your fathers, and in you their posterity.
" The wretches, who had combated Christianity,
" imagined they would find a herd of bondsmen ;
" they found the catacombs again, and they them-
" selves perished in presence of that generosity,
" that strong patience, which it pleased God to

" give us. It went harder with the Holy See than
" any other, because it is the head ; and it is the
" brow that bears every affront, as well as every
" crown.

" God took a man whom He invested with
" much power, — a man called great, but not
" great enough not to abuse his power; He set
" him in conflict for a time with that aged
" man of the Vatican, and that aged man van-
" quished him at the very climax of his triumphs.
" When the old man returned to his capital,
" Rome came out from the midst of her solitude,
" and appeared to the earth in all the majesty of
" her recovered pontificate.

" And Spain which had conquered the two
" Indies, and borne afar the standard of the faith—
" from the time of Philip II., Spain, that great
" Catholic nation, struck down by the despotism
" of that renowned monarch, had never again
" risen ; she lay like an uprooted tree which can
" never produce young and healthy foliage, but
" which is still shaded by its ancient glory, and
" its mighty arms.

" It pleased the man, of whom I was just

" speaking, to claim it in virtue of what all con-
" querors call the *right* of conquest. When told,
" ' Take care how you attack that people !' he
" replied, 'It is a nation *fashioned* by monks, and
" ' all nations fashioned by monks are cowards !'
" And at the foot of the Pyrenees, he found
" Christians formed by monks ; and his warriors,
" who used to say that from the Pyrenees to the
" Baltic they had met nothing but children, con-
" fessed, in language both military and energetic,
" that they were more than men ; that it was a
" war of giants. Spain had the signal honor of
" being the primary cause of that man's ruin, and
" of the world's deliverance."

He ended thus : " Let us form Christians in
" our schools ; but, above all, let us form Chris-
" tians in our own hearts. Children of Christ,
" be great like your Father ; be generous as the
" Cross on which you were born. The world, no
" doubt, will not know you ; but a few suffering
" souls will know you : they will learn from you
" the power and beauty of Christianity ; and in
" whatever clime or age you live, you will be of
" those who here below uphold respect for God

S

" and man : those two great respects whose union
" is the salvation of the world."

A kind of foreboding of the silence with which
he was threatened seems, for a moment, to have
gained his thoughts. "It would require no army
" here to close my mouth, a single soldier would
" be sufficient. But God has given me for the
" defence of my speech, and of the truth which
" is in it, something which can withstand all the
" empires of the earth."

Whatever be the case, from that day it became
impossible for him to preach at Paris.

Two years later, called by the duties of his
charge as provincial to Toulouse, and those countries where he came, at every step, upon monuments of the zeal and faith of his spiritual
ancestors, he was invited by the archbishop* to
resume his conferences for the numerous youth of
that intellectual metropolis of the south, which
was the cradle of St. Dominic, and the tomb of

---

* Mgr. Mioland, died in 1858.

St. Thomas Aquinas. He consequently gave six conferences there in 1854, and I venture to say they are the most eloquent, the most unblemished, of all. He considered life in every stage, life in general, the life of the passions, moral life, supernatural life, and the influence of the latter upon public and private life.

At the end of the sixth conference, he announced his intention of treating, in his future discourses, the means established by God for the communication of supernatural life, that is, the sacraments ; but this last discourse contained, upon the moral misery of nations, fallen from the high estate of political freedom, and reduced to what he called *private life*, certain outbursts of truth, grief, and offended honesty, which were out of season. He had finally to give up preaching in public.

At the end of the station of Toulouse the direction of the School of Sorèze was offered to him. He accepted it, and devoted to it and the government of the Dominican province of France the rest of his life.

In vain did two hundred young students of

the law schools of Toulouse petition him to resume his conferences for their benefit. His
answer was grateful and betrayed emotion, but
was negative. " This is not the first time that
" I have been the object of demonstrations simi-
" lar to the one with which the youth of Toulouse
" honour me; but this one touches me the more,
" since being older, I am now sinking into ob-
" livion. . . The cry of souls never left me un-
" moved, and without a desire of devoting myself.
" . . But God imposes upon me obscure duties. .
" I must love them, and forget the past." *

I do not believe that any formal prohibition,
even from the temporal power, was ever signified
to him ; but there was a kind of general feeling
that that bold and free voice, which had been
heard for twenty years, under all kinds of governments, without ever being checked, and with no
other curb than that of orthodoxy, was no longer
in place. Evil days had dawned upon the con-

---

* Letter inserted in the *Echo de l'Aude*, March 30th, 1855.

flicts and triumphs of eloquence. It was universally spurned and held accountable for all the misfortunes of the country, for all the perils of society, by a turn which was a triumph for all those who had never been able to get anyone to listen to them. The prince of sacred eloquence was condemned to silence. He has himself said so since : "I was forced to leave the pulpit by a " secret instinct of my liberty, in presence of an " age which had no longer all its own." * " I " saw," he added, " that in my ideas, in my " language, and in my past, I also was a liberty, " and that my time was come for disappearing " with the rest." †

When Lacordaire left for ever the pulpit of Notre-Dame, he was but forty-nine years old. In more than one respect, he could apply to himself the words which, a few years before, he pronounced over M. de Forbin-Janson, bishop of Nancy; words easy of application as well as

-----

* *Notice sur le Père de Ravignan.*
† Memoirs dictated on his death-bed, in October 1861.

worthy of meditation, in a country so freely given
to scorn illustrious and unmerited reverses : " He
" was forty-five years of age,—the age of pleni-
" tude, the age when all that has been sown in
" life raises around the man its shady branches
" laden with fruit ; and this very time was the
" one in which he was cut off from his past, and
" saw life before him, like a tree cut down by
" the root. It is difficult for those who have not
" experienced it to know the painfulness of this
" situation, and the amount of courage required
" to bear up under it. Mgr. de Janson did not
" sink under it, he did not contemplate his dis-
" grace without emotion and regret ; but he
" found in his heart wherewith to bear it before
" God, to honor it before men, and to turn it to
" the good of his fellows." *

The great orator had to complain of no
violence, no persecution ; and I do but state the
truth in saying that I never detected in him the

---

* Funeral Oration of Mgr. de Forbin-Janson, bishop of
Nancy, August 28th, 1844.

slightest tinge of bitterness or animosity towards the new government. That government prompted him simply to a dignified neutrality, if anything, slightly disdainful, as was his wont with regard to all governments.

But the country! public opinion, the multitude! That country which he supposed to be panting after every liberty! That opinion which he had seen so excited, so ready, not only for resistance, but for revolt! Those multitudes but lately so rebellious to all authority, even the mildest, suddenly become eager not only to accept but to cry out for a master. Alas! what a bitter disenchantment for his patriotism! And he repeatedly expressed too what he felt on the subject.

" One may have," said he, " wit, knowledge, " genius even, and still have no character. Such " is the France of to-day. She is crowded with " men who have taken everything from the hands " of fortune, and who still have betrayed nothing; " because in order to betray, you must have cared " for something.

" To them events are fleeting clouds, a show,

" a shelter, nothing more. They submit to them
" without resistance, after having unintentionally
" paved the way for them—inconsistent playthings
" of a past of which they were not masters, and
" of a future which withholds its secrets.

   " Everything breaks down before thirty mil-
" lions of men, who do not know how to stand
" by anything, and who have lost the political
" sentiment of religion and right."*

   The whole of Europe seemed to him to deserve
as severe a judgment as France. " What saddens
" one," he wrote, "is the incapacity of men to
" parry evils which everyone foresees. There is
" not a single cabinet in Europe seriously de-
" sirous of contributing to the pacification of
" Italy and the world. . . . . . . Nought, nought,
" nought, but interest, brute force, and cannon ;
" such is the only cleverness of the masters of
" the world! This madness and egotism of human
" power irritate me more than the fury of dema-

---

* *Première Lettre à un Jeune Homme sur la Vie Chrétienne,*
March 1858.

" gogy. Those people, the demagogues, have an
" apparent pretext, an inkling of an idea and of
" devotedness; they still believe in something,
" at least we may give a certain number of them
" credit for so doing; but the others! Thank
" God if we perish with the rest, we shall, at
" least, have been in none of the camps of evil."*

But what was this purely political wound in
comparison with that which pierced his priestly
heart, at the sight of the attitude taken up by
Catholics, and a too large portion of the clergy!
How should he have been otherwise than astounded
and broken-hearted? He saw that clergy and
those Catholics who had so long applauded the
manly independence of his voice, suddenly fall
a prey to an unpardonable illusion, and to a
prostration unexampled in the history of the
Church. Names which had had the honour to
figure beside his own in those memorable mani-
festoes in which Christian freedom was invoked

----

* 30th January, 1858.

under the shadow of public liberty, suddenly appeared at the foot of orations and pastorals, which borrowed the forms of Byzantine adulation in order to greet the mad dream of an orthodox absolutism.

All the cynicism of political apostasy was acted over again and outdone by the shameful ranting of the principal organs of Catholic opinion in the press : " The Ultramontane school," wrote the Archbishop of Paris,* " was but lately a school " of liberty ; it has been turned into a school of " slavery, which is attempting to bring about a " double idolatry, the idolatry of the temporal " and the idolatry of the spiritual power."

Those who had so loudly claimed common rights and liberty for all, who had so proudly paraded their contempt for the advances of power and its protection, who had so noisily insisted that they wanted rights and not places, so boldly declared that liberty was both *the cry of the*

---

* Monseigneur Sibour, letter of 10th December, 1853.

Church in its infancy, and the cry of victorious humanity, and that the people of February 1848 had the *divine sentiment* of the natural alliance between Catholicism and liberty ;* these very men cast aside like dung all the guarantees, all the institutions, all the principles of a past in which they had all been either actors or spectators. Wilfully blind, they pretended to concur in or at least to assist at the restoration of what they called Christian monarchy, and, under this pretence, they were to be seen exculpating at the same time the Roman empire and the first French empire, crying down all the rights of political liberty, loudly calling in force to the assistance of the faith, affirming that the yoke of the law of God must be forced upon all ; lauding and regretting the Inquisition ; declaring the ideal principle of liberty to be anti-Christian ; even civil tolerance to be crime ; finally, shamelessly putting forth that in claiming under Louis Philippe general liberty,

---

* Electoral profession of faith of M. l'Abbé de Salinis, (since Archbishop of Auch,) on the 5th April, 1848.

they had simply meant their own, and, " that
" liberty of conscience ought to be restricted in
" proportion as truth prevailed." *   After having
repeated to satiety, that whenever the Church was
protected they felt free, they went so far as to give
the name of *" pagan and naturalist prejudices "*†
to those principles of paternal authority and
personal liberty, in the name of which the whole
French episcopate had been for twenty years
demanding, and had at last obtained liberty of
education.

One may easily imagine the horror with which
such speedy and such black ingratitude towards
freedom was calculated to strike him, who, from
the pulpit of Notre-Dame, had, in presence of
his archbishop, and without a single Catholic
voice being raised to gainsay or warn him, thus
enunciated the language of justice and honor :—
" Whoever in his cry for right, excepts a single
" man ; whoever consents to the slavery of a

---

* *Univers*, 14th November, 1854.
† *Univers*, 24th October, 1858.

" single man, be he white or black, were it only
" to extend to the unlawful binding of a single
" hair of his head; that man is not sincere,
" and deserves not to fight for the sacred cause
" of the human race. Public conscience will
" always repel the man who asks for exclusive
" liberty, or forgets the rights of others; for
" exclusive liberty is but a privilege, and a
" liberty forgetful of others' rights is nothing
" better than treason. . . . . But there is
" in the heart of the honest man who speaks
" for all, and who, in speaking for all, sometimes
" seems to be speaking against himself, there is
" in that man a power, a logical and moral su-
" periority, which almost infallibly begets reci-
" procity. Yes, Catholics, know this well: if
" you want liberty for yourselves, you must will
" it for all men under heaven. If you ask it
" for yourselves simply, it will never be granted;
" give it where you are masters, in order that it
" may be given you there where you are slaves."

He indeed was not the man to have ever
accepted the shadow even of complicity in this
painful transformation; he who in his last inter-

view with the Catholic youth of Paris, said to them :—" I hope to live and die a penitent Catholic, and an *impenitent liberal*."*

He was not one whom the disasters of liberty could drive into the ante-room of her enemies. He had known and loved her when she was surrounded by honor and adoration, queen of opinion, and of the future. How could his generous soul have forsaken her in her defeat and humiliation!

But how, moreover, would he have been able to console himself on seeing the Catholic standard, the honor of the Church, and the whole social influence of religion, laid open to the hazards of so lamentable a change of opinion?

Everything in his noble nature must have been shocked at so unforeseen a desertion, and especially at the arrogance and audacity of the chiefs and doctors of this desertion, in setting themselves upon the majority of the clergy and the

---

* Answer to the deputation of the *Cercle* catholique, after his reception at the French Academy.

religious public as oracles, without any other warrant than the versatile bombast of their opinions, and the perfidious shrewdness of their denunciations against everybody who refused to follow them in their new evolution.

He immediately recognized the direct connection between this tyrannical school and the old school of La Mennais,—of La Mennais, the absolutist and ultramontane, so soon to become the unbeliever and revolutionary ; a school which had never pleased him, and which at the very outset revolted him by its violent diatribes against the old French clergy, to which he did not belong, but in which he loved to recognize "that great " and priestly tone, which bespoke both nobleness " of nature and the elevation of grace." "All this " madness," he said, " for liberty, after the Belgian " fashion, has then suddenly turned into a fana- " tical love of despotism, and very few have held " fast, and honored the Church by their con- " stancy."

" We are again in presence of the *Catholic* " *Memorial* of 1824 without the man of genius who " headed it ; and with the recklessness of a deser-

" tion conscious of its guilt.   God allows us, in
" these lamentable circumstances, to stand by the
" convictions of our youth and our first struggles ;
" it is a very great grace, the value of which will be
" better known only in the future.   We cannot
" take too much pains to turn it to account for
" the Church, so cruelly harassed by minds whose
" shameless excesses are the signs of unbounded
" weakness.   They think themselves the leaders
" of Christendom, and they are but a horde of
" Scythians."*

The grief and indignation felt by him at the
sight of this " great moral debasement " never
abated until the last day of his life.   He was still
more affected by it than we, since the honor of
his cloth was more compromised in it than ours,
whilst his duty as a religious, and his position as
head of an order, imposed upon him a silent
reserve to which we were not obliged.   He had to
say, like a contemporary of Galileo : " *Inter hos*

---

* Flavigny, 27th February, 1853.

" *vivendum, moriendum, et quod est durius tacen-*
" *dum!*" But his affliction, his magnanimous
anger burst forth in his letters. This treasure,
thank God, remains; it will be kept for posterity,
and when the time shall have come in which
everything may be said, it will be looked upon by
that posterity as the most signal, as well as most
necessary, of protestations against those who have
so miserably divided, disarmed, and degraded
Catholicism in France.

Let us now, however, lend an ear to a few of
his accents, which will ring in our souls like the
roars of the wounded lion.

In the very midst of their triumph these
men were thus judged by him : " They rely
" upon the fears and passions of the present
" moment ; public apostates, they have chosen
" their ground in the very centre of every re-
" action, have cloaked their own cowardice with
‘the cowardice of all, and have (in order the
more surely to deaden the sting of conscience)
" shown the most unlimited exaggeration in pro-
" claiming opinions directly opposite to those

T

" previously defended by themselves. . . . .
" They have become, like the partisans of all
" lost causes, the desperate champions and reck-
" less retailers of old doctrines the most repro-
" bated by universal opinion, and which, even
" in past times, were simply problems allowed to
" be very difficult of solution." *

" . . . . . Their style is always the same . . . .
" full of spleen and outrageous personalities. The
" whole secret of that style consists in finding
" out some insult for a substantive, and some
" other insult for an adjective. † . . . . . . Fortu-
" nately the silence of sixty-four out of eighty
" bishops will one day be a clear proof that
" all the clergy of France is not under the yoke
" of so sorry a faction. ‡ . . . . . To earn the
" hatred of such men is, to my mind, a very
" great honor, and if I am to be pitied at all,
" it is for not having been treated like M. de

---

* 18th January, 1855.
† 9th August, 1855.   ‡ 10th September, 1856.

" Falloux. I devoutly trust they will draw me " on their hurdle before I die."*

The timid and useless reserve which did so much to encourage the aggressive audacity of these false prophets, and the blindness of their followers, never met with anything but energetic reprobation from him.

" We must know how to break with men who " do harm in the name of God, and we are not to " call them *my dear friend*, under the pretext " that they are old acquaintances, and that they " go to communion every week. We must not " hate but we must separate ; and we must " especially guard against fearing those whom " we no longer deem deserving of our affection."†

This reprobation seemed to intensify as his end drew near. Already grievously stricken by disease which carried him off a few months later, he thus expressed himself :

---

* 30th January, 1858. This wish was not fulfilled until after his death. (See the *Monde* of 1st February, 1862.)

† 6th December, 1855.

" This hateful apostasy, which has been one
" of the causes of the present misfortunes of the
" Church, still continues then, although already
" severely punished. Thank God we have had
" nothing to do with it .... and nothing in the
" world affords me more consolation than this
" thought. This fact is our eternal glory, the un-
" answerable proof of our sincerity, the deep
" bond of our public friendship. We have not
" been of those who, after having claimed '*liberty*
" '*for all,—civil, political, and religious liberty*,'
" have unfurled the standard of the Inquisition,
" and of Philip the Second, shamelessly eaten
" their own words, taunted their old companions
" in arms with their steadfastness and fidelity,
" dishonored the Church, hailed Cæsar with
" acclamations that would have excited the scorn
" of Tiberius, and who to-day, despite the lesson
" taught them by events, are still, after their fall,
" parading the evil they have done, and the shame
" with which they are overwhelmed. We never
" belonged to them ; we held aloof from the
" outset. At my latest breath and in my tomb,
" this will be a pure and sweet thought to me ;

" it will be likewise the lasting token of our un-
" broken and unclouded friendship." *

I know to what I lay myself open by evoking
from the grave, against an aberration in which so
many have had a guilty hand, the terrible voice of
this great and indignant Christian.   But I make
up my mind beforehand to bear joyfully all the
recrimination to which these words, bearing the
stamp of foresight as well as of justice, may give
rise ; for the school which he thus scourged is
doing its best to secure for us the same amount of
peril and insult in the future, as it succeeded in
bringing upon us during the past.   I add that we
should have to blink every truth useful to our
contemporaries, if we could not appeal to the
authority of evidence such as that of Lacordaire,
borne out by his noble life, and backed in a still
more imposing manner by his death.

He experienced, then, in all its intensity what
he called " *le poignant chagrin des hommes et des*

---

* 13th April, 1861.

" *choses d'aujourd'hui;*" he was literally eaten up
by it. And it is not going too far to believe that
it shortened his life at least as much as his excessive austerities. Let no one reproach him with
it ; they who know not such grief are more to be
pitied than they who die of it.

Still, his irritation did not degenerate into
discouragement, and his sadness was never without hope. He used to love to seek that hope
in the memories of our ancient struggles, in the
times " in which we were yet unacquainted with
" the checks, the treason, the fickleness, and
" cowardice which have overshadowed our prime.*
" . . . . However sad," he said, " be the
" spectacle of the world to-day, we must not give
" way to despondency, which is the worst of evils.
" Hope ought to survive everything, and show it-
" self in those who deserve to hope. Their heart
" is the ark of everything yet untainted.† . . . .
" . . . . : . Nothing has left so bright a trace in

---

* 31st October, 1858.   † 29th November, 1857.

" history as those scarce specimens of human
" dignity in times of baseness.* . . . . We
" are indeed solitary ; but we are with our duty,
" and that is enough.

" God has kept us pure from all treason for
" nearly thirty years : I trust he will keep us so
" till the end.† . . . . We ought to serve the
" clergy, and not flatter it in its mistaken ten-
" dencies. The *Correspondant* is a protest against
" the false line taken up by a certain set of
" Catholics, and this protest ought to extend to
" all the social, political, literary, and scientific
" questions which may be broached around us.
" We have no popularity either to gain or to keep;
" we look only to the honor of holding the ground
" of fairness, honesty, foresight, and Christian
" good-taste. All the rest is worthless.‡

" God alone knows whether or not we shall
" see better days ; whether France deserves to
" win back, in our day, the institutions she has

---

* 6th December, 1858.   † 30th April, 1858.
‡ October 14th, 1858.

" wilfully lost. But, whatever may happen during
" our lifetime, a future will dawn upon our grave.
" It will find us pure from treason, from defection,
" from pandering to success, and firm in our hope
" of a political and religious state of things worthy
" of the Christianity whose children we are. We
" have scorned the idea of propping up our faith
" by despotism, wherever it is to be found ; we
" have looked for the triumph of that faith in
" no other arms than those used by the apostles
" and martyrs, and if that faith is to triumph over
" this world, so far gone in moral and intellectual
" disorder, it will only do so by the means which
" helped it to overthrow paganism, and which
" have, up to the present, saved it from the com-
" bined hatred of a mistaken philosophy and mis-
" taken politics."*

This public grief, which was the keenest and
longest of his life, was not the only bitterness
with which he was filled. He knew others, nearer

---

* November 26th, 1858.

home, and no less unexpected; he met with ingratitude in every shape, and with division where he had least to expect it.

Let us cast a veil over these trials, the common lot of all men, which, however, never awoke in his heart a doubt of God's justice even in this life, nor even succeeded in making him misanthropical. Still, he but slowly got the better of the grief into which he was thrown by certain miscalculations, certain desertions; he, for a time, remained stunned, and as though overwhelmed. Then, bracing himself up, and casting far behind him the remembrance, like a load which soils more than it tires, he gave himself up to the great occupation of his latter years, the education of youth.

"One of the consolations of my present life," said he, "is to live only with God and children; "the latter have their faults, but they have as "yet betrayed and dishonored nothing."*

God allowed him to find at Sorèze the laborious and stirring retirement which he needed.

---

* Letter of 11th October, 1854.

This ancient abbey, founded in 757 by Pepin le Bref, was changed a thousand years later into a military college, kept by the Benedictines. After a century of new and striking vicissitudes, it fell to the third order of St. Dominic, which Lacordaire had just re-organized by adapting it to the education of youth, which had always been the supreme vocation of his life.

He settled down at Sorèze in 1854, the year in which he finally gave over preaching, after having devoted twenty years to this task. In order to regenerate this great school he wanted to conduct, animate, and govern everything in person; he succeeded beyond all expectation; and when, in 1857,* he celebrated its more than millenary jubilee, he had already made it the most

---

* We may refer our readers to the very interesting account of this solemnity, published in the *Correspondant* of 25th September, 1857, vol. xlii., p. 37. Upon an obelisk in the play-ground of the school Lacordaire had engraved this characteristic inscription :

Primum scholæ sæculum
Post decem abbatiæ sæcula.

flourishing and popular scholastic establishment of the South.

Here it was that the suffrages of the French Academy* were to follow him, and confer upon him the noblest reward, which, in our days, can crown a glorious and independent life. Thence it was that he was to come and take his place, for one single day, in the ranks of that illustrious assembly, and personify, as he said in its presence, " the symbol of liberty accepted and strengthened " by religion."

Hither it was that he was to go back and die. He had already chosen his burial-place. " Sorèze," said he, condensing his thought in three Latin words, " will be the tomb of my " life, the asylum of my death, and a benefit " to both. *Viventi sepulchrum, morienti hospitium,* " *utrique beneficium.*"

The close of his career was, by this laborious

---

task of teaching, linked with the beginning;
when, asked by the Chancellor before the Court
of Peers what was his profession, he replied *a
schoolmaster.**

But that which attracted him and held him to
Sorèze until his last breath was the love of youth,
that predominant passion of his soul, and in his
eyes the surest way to serve God and one's neigh-
bour. A constant witness of his last struggles
has told us that this generous passion seemed to
give him a certain uneasiness, during the throes
of his agony : " Some movement of self-love may
" have glided into my actions, but I was unaware
" of it; I do think that I have always desired
" to serve God, the Church . . . . . ." His voice
failed, then he continued with force : " and our
" Lord Jesus Christ . . . . . I have loved youth

---

* The Count de Montalembert's own reply was, if possible, more characteristic, and shows with what honest ardour
he had thrown himself into this great struggle. When asked
the same question, he replied, "*A schoolmaster and a peer of
France.*"—[*Translator's Note.*]

" much, yes, very much ; but could our good
" God reproach me with it ?"*

For youth then, so dear to him, he was for the
future to reserve the treasures of his soul and his
eloquence.

In his account of his first relations with
Ozanam he has depicted, with that depth and
freshness of coloring which never failed him, the
charming bond which is formed between a young
soul just opening to the first dawn of enthusiasm,
and the man of celebrity, especially the priest,
who opens to him his door and his heart.

" The first visits of a young man to men not
" of his own age, who have preceded him in life,
" and from whom he hopes, without well knowing
" why, for a kindly reception, are an event.
" Hitherto he has seen nothing but the caresses
" of his family and the familiarity of his com-
" panions; he has not seen man ; he has not
" made that sorrowful shore where the waves

---

* *Dernière Maladie et Mort du R. P. Lacordaire,* par le R. P.
Mourey, directeur de l'école de Sorèze, p. 23.

" throw up so many bitter plants and work such
" deep furrows ; he is unconscious and trustful.
" Ozanam was unconscious and trustful. Besides
" I was not merely a man for him, I was a priest ;
" the child who has unbosomed himself to a priest
" feels sweetly drawn towards him, and what wo-
" man is to the heart buffeted by the passions, the
" priest is to the heart that is striving to become
" pure."

But to how many others had he not been
what he was to Ozanam? And when after
these fatherly and intimate conversations the
champion of the great oratorical tourneys breathed
again the breath of conflict and public speech, it
was still for his dear youths that he wrote and
delivered, on the scholar feasts, those discourses,
finished productions, in which his eloquence
" flows in upon the soul like a river of unction
" and peace," and in which he studies to instil
into them at one time the sentiment and love of
work and devotedness,* at another to teach them

---

* Discourse of 7th April, 1855, *Œuvres*, f. v., p. 833.

the rights and duties of property,* at another to vindicate before them philosophy from the outrage done it, in the proscription, of its very name, from the programme of official studies.†

These solemn occasions were not the only ones upon which they enjoyed the benefit of his habitual eloquence. He preached every week in the college chapel, and the most trustworthy witnesses assure us that he preached to that young audience with the same care and the same love as when he was listened to by the multitude. The same fire, the same vehemence, the same transports were there as at Notre-Dame.

During the last Lent of his life, already worn out by his mortal sickness, he was still faithful to that exhausting custom. He chose for the subject of his familiar conferences *Duty* : he led these children from stage to stage through the ranks of all those who do their duty, and whom

---

* Discourse of 11th April, 1858, *Correspondant*, v. xlv. p. 1.

† Discourse of 10th April, 1859, upon Philosophical Studies, *Correspondant*, vol. xlvii.

he thus classed in a magnificent hierarchy,—the honest man, the man of honor, the magnanimous man, the hero, the saint! But lassitude and suffering had already forced him to discontinue confessing the pupils, which he looked upon as one of his dearest and most sacred duties.

I owe it to him to relate, that one day when I wanted to keep him in Paris for an important and delicate reason, he answered after some little hesitation, " No, I cannot, it would perhaps " prevent some of my children who are preparing " for the coming festival from going to confession. " No one can say what the loss of one com- " munion may be in the life of a Christian." And he immediately travelled six hundred miles in order not to deprive his children of the aid of his spiritual paternity. He thus acquired the right to tell them, in the last allocution he addressed them with a faltering voice shortly before his death : " If my sword has gone rusty, " gentlemen, it is in your service."

It was for them that he conceived the plan, and laid the basis of the great and last edifice he intended raising, and in which he wanted to treat the practical side of religion in his *Lettres à un Jeune Homme sur la Vie Chrétienne.*

He was repeatedly pressed to take advantage of his retirement for writing purposes. Many subjects were suggested to him ; but he had very little taste for purely literary ˙ labors, and for too frequent publications. This repugnance dated from his youth. " I hate many books," he said. " The greatest men have, out of sixty volumes, " not left more than two or three readable works, " and at bottom this small number contains all " their thought. After the lapse of two centuries, " but very few of the books written in past times " are read, and frequently it is the man's life " which gets his books a reading. The memory " of the man preserves his works from oblivion. " The capital point is to have *an aim in life*, and " deeply to respect posterity, by sending it but " a small number of well-meditated writings."*

To have an aim in life: this programme had

---

* Rome, 13th August, 1837.

U

undoubtedly been well filled up by Lacordaire : one
is moved to see, at the close of his life, the love of
souls inspire him with an increase of zeal, and
impose upon him an increase of toil in the service
of that youth to which he was desirous of im-
parting lessons more familiar and practical even
than during the past.

His first idea was to make them the subject of
a series of discourses, but no longer seeing any
possibility of resuming his apostolic labors;
whether on account of the times, or of his scholastic occupations ; he chose the epistolary form.*

---

* On beginning this series, he wrote to me on January
30th, 1858 :—" This will be a lengthy affair, for I imagine
" my plan will take up no less than from sixty to eighty letters,
" of two octavo sheets each, which would make up from three
" to four volumes. It is by this that I will end my career, and
" shall thus, if God wills it, have published before my death a
" complete body of apologetic and moral theology." Later on,
he reduced his plan.   In a note dictated to me, on the 27th
of September, 1861, from the bed from which he was not
again to rise, although unaware of the proximity of death, he
said he thought he would devote but from thirty to thirty-five
letters to it.   The three first (the only ones either published
or written), on the Worship of Jesus Christ, as founder of the

He hesitated before handing over these letters
to publicity. "With regard to the substance of
"the work," said he, "I have quite made up my
"mind: none would be more analogous to my
"previous works; none would better complete
"them; none even could be more useful.......
"Christian life is a scarcity to-day even among
"Christians. The decline of character, the shaki-
"ness of convictions, the likeness between every
"life and every other life, would seem to prove
"that the grandeur of the Gospel does not stamp
"itself powerfully enough upon souls. Can this
"not be remedied in a certain number? The
"Jansenists, under Louis XIV., tried it, and, to

Christian life in the Scriptures and in the Church, were to be
followed by a fourth upon the Worship of *Jesus Christ* in *priests,
the bishops, and the pope*: this was what he called the vestibule
of the work. Then followed three great divisions or categories
of letters, destined to treat of the worship of Jesus Christ;
firstly, in the virtues; secondly, in the sacraments; thirdly,
in the mysteries, and in the liturgy. Each category would
have comprised from ten to twelve letters, each of about forty
pages; and the whole was to form the matter of about three
volumes.

" a certain degree, succeeded ; but the error of
" their dogmatic starting-point prevented them
" from a healthy and strong tradition. Still,
" since their fall, there has been a great void.
" Lax morality has penetrated everywhere ; it
" has lowered many things, and many men, even
" among the clergy. The clergy is, perhaps, more
" in want of a certain interior spring than of
" theological knowledge or social convictions."*

True to this programme, he poured forth,
in the only three letters he had the time to
publish, the real Christian sap, and in them,
as well as in two articles of his upon the Prince
de Broglie's book, his thought and style both
reached their culminating point : one reads them
over and over again with ever increasing emotion.
All the blemishes of his former writings, which
rose to the surface like the dross of a precious
metal in ebullition, have disappeared. Both as
to matter and form, there remains nothing but

---

* Sorèze, December 15th, 1857.

grandeur, elevation, force, and originality of genius. By the rarest of privileges he preserves there the energy and dash, the very graces of youth, whilst, at the same time, he displays all the perfection and authority which maturity lends to intellectual gifts.

Madame Swetchine, whom we must quote for the last time, was right in saying, " The splendour " of his eloquence is ever on the rise, and its " beauty is incomparable; never was talent seen " ripening under more brilliant conditions, which " seem to belong exclusively to youth."*

May I be allowed to add, that, looking out as I always do for what reveals, in great lives, the man, the inmost fibre of the heart, what, to me, seems most attractive in Lacordaire is that modesty, that distrust of self, which becomes man at all times, but which awakes the deepest emotion when met with at the decline of life, and in one who has achieved glory.

---

* Letter of 8th September, 1856, to the Countess de Mesnard, vol. ii., p. 393.

"It is now more than thirty years," he says to his Emmanuel, "since, young like your- "self, thrown like you into contact with the "revelations of one of this world's great cities, "I lifted for the first time a timid look towards "the goodness of God. Since that time I have "never ceased to believe and to love. Years, true "to their mission, have daily brought me greater "certainty, more divine joys, and I have seen "man diminish in my eyes, whilst Christ gra- "dually grew upon me. You are then knocking "at a door which opens of itself; you are "touching a fruit which falls of itself; and that "is precisely what draws me most towards you.

"I ask myself whether it be not too late; "whether I have time enough before me to "instruct you, or whether the weakness of age, "unequal to the ardour of conviction, will leave "me what I require to sow in you the grain "of eternity; or rather that grain is within "you, since faith resides in you: but what a "distance from faith to love, and from love in "the bud to love in its full bloom!

"I am an old vessel, and I fear for you who

" want to drink out of it ; still, may God assist
" me, and his grace, after having prepared it,
" sustain your heart !" *

Farther on it is confidence mingled with
tenderness, that is uppermost : " On the verge
" of decline, I love to talk to you, no longer of
" the deep mysteries of dogma, but of the familiar
" mysteries of life. When young, one loves to
" brave vague perils ; later, when the length of
" the journey has already matured the heart, and
" calmed the intellect, one comes back with joy
" to the quiet of home ; one feels the value of
" resting upon what is already acquired ; and the
" approach of death reveals to us, sweetly and
" noiselessly, more mysteries than speculation
" discloses to genius itself.

" You are coming, and I am going ; it is a
" consolation to those who are leaving to embrace
" those who are staying behind, and the thought
" of those who are gone is the strength of those
" who are left.

---

* *Correspondant* of 25th March, p. 383.

" I will rekindle my breath at the flame of
" yours, and you, the child of an agitated age,
" which was once mine, will perhaps catch in my
" fire, smouldering but not dead, something which
" will give you fervour and peace."

The Emmanuel to whom he addressed such
sweet and deep lessons, was no imaginary inter-
locutor; he was a young Christian, made up of
flesh and blood, a pupil who had left Sorèze, and
whom the master had marked out amongst all, as
the depositary of his last and tenderest communications. These new ties did not render him
unfaithful to any one of the old friends who
remained worthy of him.

To one of them, whom betimes he considered
too impassioned, and too much mixed up in current affairs, he said in his usually charming way:
" We meet in the calmer and more universal
" region of ideas and principles, like trees, whose
" roots are far apart, but whose tops meet and
" interweave, forming but a single shade in the
" light which surrounds them both alike."

But who would not have envied his having
found, against the chill which age but too often

brings with it, a remedy in these youthful ardours ? His heart, tender and expansive as in the first days of his youth, was always seeking out other hearts to love. He had been tempted to adopt, in a special way, one of his pupils at Sorèze, in order to take exclusively upon himself the care of his education.

" I would have made him the child of my soul, " I should have made myself over to him as a gift. " If I have not taken to myself a child, it is not " because I have been dissuaded by the fear of " seeing him die in the midst of my efforts, or at " the moment when he would have been able to " turn them to account. Everything belongs to " God, and in offering up to Him this death, I " should have made the most meritorious of sac- " rifices. But I feared ingratitude. . . . I should " have loved him so much, that had he been un- " faithful to my love in God, he would have tried " too severely the weakness of my human nature."*

---

* Conversation of the 11th of October, 1857, noted down by M. F. Lacointa, *Revue de Toulouse*, 1st January, 1862.

This is indeed he! After the lapse of thirty years I find him just the same as he appeared to me in his first conversations, and in his first letters, when he wrote to me : " I will never " believe that the heart can wear out, and I feel " every day that it becomes stronger, more tender, " more detached from the ties of the body, in " proportion as life and reflection neutralize the " covering in which it is stifled. . . . . The heart " may die by killing the body ; this is the only " end I will admit for it, but it is the end of a " combat crowned by victory."*

It is with no less emotion that, in the midst of this passionate ardour for good, for the conquest and salvation of souls, I hear vibrating the un-dying chord of that melancholy which had gently pursued him, even in his youth. Whilst yet a seminarist, he said : " I am sad betimes, but who " is there that is not so ? It is a dart which we " must always carry in the soul ; we must try not

---

* 13th March, 1832.

" to lean on the side where it is, without ever
" thinking of taking it out. It is the javelin of
" Mantinea in the breast of Epaminondas; it is
" extracted only by death and entrance into
" eternity."*

His glorious career opens, is run, and closes;
and, although as yet far from the goal, we still
hear the echo of a complaint softened by faith:
" When a life has been spent in unselfish toil,
" and, at the end of a career, we see the difficulty
" of every thing here below get the upper hand
" of desires and efforts, then the soul, without
" eschewing good, experiences the bitterness of
" unrequited sacrifice, and turns towards God in
" a melancholy which virtue may condemn, but
" which divine goodness must forgive."†

Yes, it will indeed be pardoned, for in him
that bitterness never degenerated into unhealthy
rancour, dark and brooding discouragement:

---

* Letter to M. Lorain, *Correspondant*, vol. xxvii., p. 836.

† Article on the work of the Prince de Broglie. *Correspondant* of 25th September, 1856.

it was ennobled and purified by a tide of poetry
and charity, as may be seen in the peroration
of one of his speeches at the distribution of prizes
at Sorèze :

"M. de Chateaubriand, bending under the
"weight of glory and of years, was one day
"on the solitary banks of the Lido, at the ex-
"tremity of the Venetian lagoons. The heavens,
"the sea, the air, the islet-shores, the horizon
"of Italy, all appeared such as the poet had been
"wont to admire them of old. It was that same
"Venice with her cupolas rising up out of the
"water; the same lion of St. Mark with its
"famous inscription, '*Peace to thee, Mark, my*
"'*Evangelist.*' It was the same splendour dimmed
"by defeat and servitude, but borrowing from the
"very ruins an imperishable charm: it was, in
"fine, the same spectacle, the same noise, the
"same silence, the East and the West united on
"one glorious spot at the foot of the Alps,
"lighted up by all the memories of Greece and of
"Rome. Still the old man became pensive and
"sad ; he could not believe that that was Venice,

" the Venice of his youth which had so moved
" him; and understanding that it was himself
" alone who was no longer the same, he whispered
" to the sea-breeze, which sighed to him in vain,
" this melancholy complaint, 'The wind which
" 'blows upon a hoary head blows from no happy
" 'shore!'

" As for me, in presence of a scene which was
" my first initiation to public life, I do not,
" despite the difference of age, experience so
" cruel a disenchantment; it seems to me as
" though my youth were being renewed in that
" which surrounds me; and, at the sound of your
" applause for our happy conquerors, at the
" thought of the deep and exquisite joys which
" await so many mothers, I will say to myself
" consoled and happy, 'The wind that blows upon
" 'a hoary head does sometimes blow from a
" 'happy shore!'"*

Consoled and happy! Such we fain would be

---

* Speech at the distribution of prizes, 7th April, 1856.

whilst listening to him. But where did he learn
the secret of that contentedness, so rare at the
decline of life and at the approach of old age.
Let us say it candidly, it was neither in the heart
of those mothers, nor in that of his dear young
friends : it was in the heart of Jesus Christ. It
is there especially that we must look for him ; it is
the love of Jesus Christ, which, after having fired
his masculine and victorious eloquence at Notre-
Dame, gushes forth from his soul in the last
effusions of his genius, and bears him aloft even
higher than of old in his grand and incomparable
flight.

" There is a day when, at the corner of a
" street, or in a lonely path, you stop short, you
" listen, and a voice whispers to your conscience :
" Here is Jesus Christ! Heavenly moment when,
" after so many beauties tried and found wanting,
" the soul discovers the only beauty which does
" not deceive! Those who have not seen it may
" put it down as a dream, but those who have
" can never forget it. Whilst in all other contem-
" plation, the light, how pure soever, falls upon

" frail and corruptible beings ; here the light is
" eternal, the object unchangeable. Whilst age
" and the slightest of accidents imperil our dearest
" friendships, the love of God in Jesus Christ
" gathers strength from our very misfortunes and
" our weakness. It may be lost at the verge of
" boyhood, because it is through another that we
" have conceived it, in the lap of our mother ; but
" when once we have made it our own, when once
" it has become the fruit of our experience in
" manhood, nothing can ever again take away
" from its firmness and its warmth. It replaces
" what is falling away and fading in us each day.
" It lives in our ruins to prop them up, in our
" forlornness to console us, and when we touch
" at the hoary summit of life, at the regions of
" ice that does not melt, it is our last warmth and
" our last breath. Our eyeballs are sightless, but
" we can still weep, and these tears are for the
" God who wept over us."*

---

* Fifth Conference of Toulouse, p. 165.

The reader will bear with another quotation ; it will be the last :

" Who shall tell you what the love of Jesus
" Christ is, if you have never known it ; and if
" you have, but for a single instant, tasted it, who
" shall recount to you its unutterable effect ? Not
" the transports of pride in the day of its greatest
" triumphs, nor the fascination of the flesh in the
" hour of its most deceitful delights, nor the
" mother receiving a son from the hands of God,
" nor the bridegroom leading his bride into the
" chaste abode of nuptial bliss, nor the poet in
" the first flight of his genius, nor anything that
" is or has been, affords an image or a shadow, or
" even an inkling of what the love of Jesus Christ
" is in a soul. Everything else is either too much
" or too little. Jesus Christ alone has the measure
" of our being ; He alone has made of greatness
" and lowliness, of strength and of unction, of
" life and death, a drink such as our heart yearned
" for without knowing it ; and those who have
" once tasted this cup, in the day of their man-
" hood, know that I speak the truth, and that

" it is an intoxication* from which there is no "͵recovery."†

We will stop here. No one expects me to have the courage to tell the last struggles, the long agony which ushered that great soul into true life. Still, I saw him, that dear and courageous sufferer, on his bed of sickness, battling in the last gripe of the disease which had been sapping his strength for the last two years, and which, at its outset, had snatched from that doughty warrior, unable to continue his wonted austerities and macerations, this cry of generous impatience, " *This is the first time that my body* " *has withstood my will.*" I saw him exhausted, —alarmed at being obliged to submit to the yoke of that body which he had fought down,—dis-

---

* This bold but happy figure involuntarily reminds us of a verse of the exquisite " Stabat Mater," said to have been the last words articulated by the immortal Walter Scott:—

> Fac me plagis vulnerari,
> Fac me cruce *inebriari*
> Et cruore filii.
>
> —[*Translator's Note.*]

† *Première Lettre à un Jeune Homme sur la Vie Chrétienne.*

x

sembling almost beyond human strength his tortures,—stifling every wail and every murmur
under a countenance shrunk up with pain; thus
maintaining to the end the manly stamp of his
faith, his eloquence, and his soul. All that great
fire of fancy and enthusiasm seemed quenched,
except the flame of his eye ; or, rather all was
still alive, but hidden under a great and solemn
silence. He spent hours together with his eyes
fixed upon the crucifix. ."I am unable to pray
" to Him ; but I look upon Him."*

If he broke this silence, it was to testify his
resignation to the will of God, and the entire
detachment of his heart, which he had always
looked upon as the groundwork of his spiritual
life.†

Whilst looking upon this giant, vanquished,

---

* Word said to M. l'Abbé Perreyve.
† " The groundwork of every spiritual edifice is detachment
" of heart: I am constantly seeing it proved. Neither birth,
" nor fortune, nor talent, nor genius, no, nothing is of greater
" worth than a detached heart."—*Letter quoted by F. Chocarne.*

prostrate, gasping, speechless, on his monastic bed, one felt obliged to repeat with the Apostle, " *Licet is qui foris est noster homo corrumpatur,* " *tamen is qui intus est renovatur de die in diem.*"

But why dwell upon this ? The story of this agony has been traced with as much respect as tenderness by one of his dearest disciples, Father Chocarne, Prior of St. Maximin.*

All those who loved Father Lacordaire have read it, and all I am sure wept whilst reading it. They there saw him wrapt till the last moment in that devotion to the passion of Jesus Christ which he preferred to all others: " You have " always loved Jesus Christ crucified, father, " have you not ?" said one of the assistants on presenting the crucifix to him. " Oh yes," he replied, whilst kissing the cross of his God.

Next to his crucified God his departing soul seems to have especially begged the help of her whom the Gospel associates with the mother of

---

* *Les Derniers Moments du Père Lacordaire, par un Religieux de l'Ordre des Frères-Prêcheurs*, Paris et Toulouse, 1861.

God in the mysteries of the passion and resurrection, of that Magdalen whose Provençal sanctuary, restored and encircled by a white crown of sixty Dominicans, was his last work ; Magdalen whom he had beforehand chosen for the guardian of the last days of his life, when it should be given him " to break with her at the feet of Jesus Christ " the frail but faithful vessel of his thought."*

We know what were his last words, " *My* " *God! open to me, open to me!* " One can scarcely imagine any better suited to the valiant soul which was leaving this world to knock at the door of a happy eternity.

It is not my business to draw from this life or this death the weighty teachings of the

---

* " As for me, who, although unworthy, have brought
" back to the mountain and temple the ancient soldiery, to
" whom Providence has given the task of watching there day
" and night, may I here write my last lines, and, like Mary
" Magdalen the day but one before the Passion, break at the
" feet of Jesus Christ this frail but faithful vessel of my
" thought."—Last lines of his book on St. Mary Magdalen,
published in 1860.

Christian pulpit. I am not writing a funeral
oration, but simply the narrative of a witness.
It will be allowed that I have spoken as little
as possible, in order to let him speak whom we
never tired of hearing, and whom we shall never
hear more.

I have enchased a few pearls of more than
earthly beauty in a poor and modest mounting,
very unworthy of them, but perhaps on that account better suited to throw up their dazzling
whiteness. Whilst praising him I feel satisfied I
have looked to truth far more than to my tender
and faithful affection, that I have in nowise over-
stepped the bounds which he himself marked out
when speaking of a holy and cherished soul :
" Whilst a man is still living, modesty ought to
" veil his acts, and friendship itself ought to be
" restrained by decency: but death is admirable in
" that it gives memory, as well as judgment, all its
" liberty, by removing those whom it strikes from
" the peril both of frailty and envy; it allows those
" who have seen to lift the veil, those who have re-
" ceived to acknowledge the gift, those who have
" loved to unbosom themselves."

And now, what will remain of him upon this
earth? I have said so, and I believe it, that his
glory will be great in a distant future. But between this and then who knows ? He will doubtless meet with the same fate as all those who,
more than others, have undergone the action of
their day, and left its stamp upon their writings
or their sayings. He will meet with the same as
greater than he—Dante, Shakespeare, Corneille :
the stamp of his age will not be wholly allowed
by subsequent ages. Certain parts of his genius
will be again disputed. Certain forms of his eloquence will go out of date. The ideas, passions,
and struggles which stirred him, will appear an-
tiquated or insignificant. The immortal truths of
religion which he upheld, sneered at by fresh enemies, or endangered by fresh folly, will require
new proofs and new champions. His foundations,
already threatened by cupidity, will perhaps be
handed over by informers to persecution and ruin.

But what neither time, nor the injustice of
man, nor the " treachery of glory," will ever take
from him, is the greatness of his character, the
honour of having been the most manly, the most

finely tempered, the most naturally heroic soul of our times; it is the having understood and practised, as no one before him ever did, that indispensable alliance between faith and liberty which alone can raise up modern society; it is the having blended, with so much strength and glory, that deep tenderness and sweet melancholy which move and attract more than genius. He will always, as he was during his life, be still more beloved than admired; and no one will look through history upon that proud and free figure without feeling a tear rising, that lowly involuntary tear, which is the seal of real glory and true love.

When I look around for one greater, one more eloquent than he, I can only think of Bossuet; and when I open Bossuet, I find in him a saying which sums up the life of our friend: I see it resplendent " with that divine brightness which is " within us, and in which we discover, as in a " globe of light, the immortal charm of honour " and virtue."

Some may, perhaps, feel an interest in reading the list of the peers of France, who sat during the trial of the Free School, and whose names, in the order of their creation, are to be found at the bottom of the verdicts of the 15th and 19th of September, 1831. I publish this list as a homage to the memory of so many illustrious personages, and honest men, who, whilst ruling according to the letter of a law which bound them, still showed the liberal spirit which animated them, by the smallness of the fine to which we were sentenced, and by the unfettered liberty of defence allowed to us :—

MM.

Le baron Pasquier, président.
Le duc de Gramont.
Le duc de Duras.
Le duc de Choiseul.
Le duc de Broglie.
Le duc de Montmorency.
Le duc de la Force.
Le maréchal duc de Tarente.
Le maréchal duc de Reggio.
Le comte du Puy.
Le marquis de Jaucourt.
Le comte Klein.
Le comte Lemercier.
Le comte Péré.

MM.

Le marquis de Sémonville.
Le duc de Castries.
Le duc de Brissac.
Le marquis d'Aligre.
Le marquis de Boissy du Coudray.
Le comte de Contades.
Le marquis de Castellane.
Le duc de Crillon.
Le comte Compans.
Le comte de Durfort.
Le comte d'Haussonville.
Le marquis de Lauriston.
Le duc de Périgord.

MM.

Le comte Molé.
Le marquis de Mathan.
Le marquis de Mun.
Le marquis d'Orvilliers.
Le marquis de Raigecourt.
Le marquis de Rougé.
Le marquis d'Osmond.
Le comte de Noé.
Le duc de Massa.
Le duc de Dalberg.
Le duc Decazes.
Le comte Lecoulteux de Canteleu.
Le comte Becker.
Le comte Raymond de Bérenger
Le comte Claparède.
Le comte Chaptal.
Le comte Cornudet.
Le marquis de Dampierre.
Le vicomte d'Houdetot.
Le marquis de Dreux-Brézé.
Le baron Mounier.
Le comte Mollien.
Le comte de Pontécoulant.
Le comte Rampon.
Le vice-amiral comte Verhuell.
Le vice-amiral comte Truguet.
Le marquis d'Angosse.

MM.

Le comte d'Hunolstein,
Le prince duc de Poix.
Le comte de Montesquiou,
Le comte de Lavillegontier,
Le baron Dubreton.
Le comte Bastard de l'Estang.
Le marquis de Pange.
Le comte Fabre (de l'Aude).
Le marquis de Vence.
Le duc de Valmy.
Le duc de Coigny.
Le baron de Beurnonville.
Le comte Siméon.
Le comte Roy.
Le comte de Vaudreuil.
Le comte de Saint-Priest.
Le comte de Tascher.
Le marquis de Mortemart.
Le maréchal comte Molitor.
Le comte Bordesoulle.
Le baron de Glandèves.
Le comte Chabrol de Crousol.
Le comte de Tournon.
Le comte d'Haubersaert.
L'amiral baron Duperré.
Le marquis Barthélemy.
Le comte d'Orglandes.
Le comte de Vogüé.
Le comte Dejean.
Le comte de Richebourg.

MM.

Le vicomte Dode de la Bru-
nerie.

Le comte Davous.

Le marquis de Maleville.

Le duc de Feltre.

Le comte de Montalivet.

Le comte du Cayla.

Le Comte de Sussy.

Le comte Cholet.

Le comte de Boissy d'Anglas.

Le comte Lanjuinais.

MM.

Le marquis de Latour du
Pin-Montauban.

Le marquis de Laplace.

Le Duc de la Rochefoucauld.

Le comte Clément de Ris.

Le comte Abrial.

Le comte de Sesmaisons.

Le duc de Richelieu.

Le comte de Sainte-Suzanne.

Le marquis d'Aux-Lally.

Le comte Herwyn de Nevele.